PENELOPE HOLT

POLLY WANTS a Lover

Women who Want : book 1

Polly Wants a Lover
Copyright © 2024 Penelope Holt
All rights reserved.

ISBN: (ebook) 978-1-964636-23-8
(print) 978-1-964636-41-2

Inkspell Publishing
207 Moonglow Circle #101
Murrells Inlet, SC 29576

Edited By Toni Kelley
Cover Art By Fantasia Frog Designs

DEDICATION

For the ones I love

PENELOPE HOLT

CHAPTER 1: CAUGHT

Polly checked the time—2:00 p.m. She'd seen Christian and the blonde go into the bar over an hour ago. They still hadn't come out. She couldn't hang around much longer. She was scheduled to give a dance class in thirty minutes, and even if she left this second, she'd have to drive pedal to metal to make it back to the studio in time. Finally, at 2:04 p.m., right as she was about to give up and leave, the door of the Oasis bar suddenly opened, and Christian emerged with his blonde companion. When they'd entered earlier, the pair had seemed all business, but now they looked decidedly cozier, and Christian was definitely more handsy. Polly watched as her husband slid his palm down the back of the blonde's coral silk blouse, over her slim waist to rest where the fabric of her gray pencil skirt pulled tight across her curvy butt.

Looks like the beers have loosened you up, Polly thought, as she crouched down in the driver's side seat of her car. The blonde reached up and put both arms around Christian's neck, lifting one foot in its high-heeled shoe off the ground. She raised her chin, seeking his lips with her own. Polly witnessed her husband look furtively from side to side to see if anyone was watching. She ducked down further, though she doubted he could spot her. She'd parked at the far end of a row in a space where she could see but not be seen. She held her breath to keep a wave of hurt from washing over her. Right before her eyes, she watched the man she loved make out with a woman she hadn't known existed until today. She saw him playfully cap off their long kiss by biting the woman's bottom lip, before escorting her across the lot to where they had parked their cars side by side. Chris got in his Jeep and took off, but the blonde lingered. Polly shifted in her seat, squinting to watch her husband's mistress apply a fresh coat of lipstick to replace the one Christian had kissed off. When she'd finished her touch-up, the blonde checked her phone, then started her BMW X3 and pulled out of the parking space.

Polly knew it was a bad idea, but she had to follow. "Okay, Blondie, who are you and where are you headed?" she muttered, as she started her Subaru and began slowly trailing her rival through the parking lot. Keeping a safe distance, she only hit the gas when the BMW made a quick left onto the main road, right as the light changed. Too intent on the chase and her runaway thoughts, Polly didn't notice the stop sign and sped through it. A sudden loud and urgent car horn startled her and she instinctively slammed on her brakes, managing to slow her Subaru enough that when it hit the oncoming pick-up truck her airbag didn't deploy. Shoot! She got out of her vehicle at the same time the other driver leapt out of his to examine his fender.

Polly held up both hands in surrender. No contest, she was the guilty party. "Sorry, sorry. My fault, I know." She glanced over and in a quick second became mesmerized by the vision before her. A tall, muscular male specimen in tight jeans, chambray cotton shirt, and work boots, made his way toward her. He started to say something, probably along the lines of 'Why the hell can't you watch where you're going?' which she absolutely deserved. Instead, his lips curved upward, revealing a spectacular smile. Polly leaned over to examine the damage. The pick-up's front fender was already marred with a few dents, so it was hard to tell which, if any, were a result of the collision. Her Subaru, however, was a different matter. The passenger-side fender was crumpled and the headlight broken. "How's your truck?" Polly asked, knowing full well he could easily claim against her insurance for any existing damage he decided to blame on her. The guy ran his hand along the shiny metal, his long, strong fingers feeling its ripples, pits, and small dents. "Doesn't look like anything much on mine, but yours is pretty banged up," he said, eyeing the smashed plastic of her bumper.

Polly sighed. "No one to blame but myself. So, do you want my insurance information?"

"Nah, you're good," he said.

Polly detected a hint of pity in his voice, along with a slight southern accent. He nodded toward her bumper. "You might be better off just getting a good body shop to work that out for you. Leave your insurance out of it. Could be cheaper that way."

"You sure you're okay with that? I know it was my fault," Polly offered. The benevolent stranger nodded. Hit with a wave of relief, Polly caught a loose lock of her black hair blowing in the summer breeze and tucked it behind her ear. She lifted a hand to shield her green eyes from the afternoon sun and looked toward the main road. She hoped to spot the blonde, but she was long gone. *Looks like you busted up my marriage and my car,* she thought to herself. Turning her attention back to the victim of her careless driving, she suddenly became aware of a flutter in her stomach, as she took in more of his appeal. Maybe a hair under six foot, he was slim but with a muscular build, dark curly hair, deep blue eyes, and a slight scruff on his strong jaw. Cute. Very cute.

"Listen," Polly said, "let me give you my number in case you change your mind and need to reach me." The guy pulled out his phone from his back pocket, then pulled up the number pad and handed it to her. She keyed in her number and passed it back to him. She held out her other hand. "I'm Polly."

"Marcus." He shook her outstretched hand with a firm grip. "Look, I'm sorry you got the worst of it. A Subaru is no match for a pick-up."

Polly checked the time again, 2:20 p.m. There was no way she'd make it back in time to give the private dance lesson. She'd just have to pray Maria hadn't left the studio and could cover for her. She had to get going. "Marcus, thanks for doing me a solid. I appreciate it."

"No problem." He smiled, then walked around the Subaru and opened the driver's side door for her. This small, chivalrous act charmed her. "Thanks," she said, sliding in behind the wheel. When she pulled away, he slapped the Subaru's roof twice as a send-off. Waiting for the light to turn green, Polly looked in her rearview mirror to see Marcus. He looked ruggedly handsome, as he stood next to his pick-up truck, watching her drive off. A couple of miles down the road, she heard the familiar ping of an incoming text.

Marcus- Hi Polly, it's Marcus.

Again, she felt a tell-tale flutter in her stomach as she scanned his message.

Marcus- Sorry about what happened. I've got a friend who works at a body shop. He could do the work for a good price. Let me know if you need his name.

Polly stopped at a drive-thru to order a coffee. She dialed the studio. "Hello, Maria? Thank goodness you're still there. I need you to cover my private lesson with the Parkers."

"No need. They called earlier to cancel," Maria informed her. "Where you at?"

"Great! I'm over in Portchester. I got into a fender bender."

Maria gasped. "No way! You okay? How bad was the other vehicle? Were they hurt?" she asked, worried.

"Yeah, I'm fine. We're both fine. His truck barely had a scratch. My Subaru, on the other hand, didn't get off so lucky," Polly said with a sigh. "Don't worry, it's still drivable. I've got a full schedule tomorrow, so I'll be in early."

"Okay. Glad everyone is okay. Later." Maria hung up.

***

On the ride home, Polly thought about the distressing scene she'd witnessed outside the bar. The accident in the parking lot with the handsome pick-up driver had distracted her from the upset that was finally starting to wash over her. Christian was cheating on her. And worse than that. *No,* she thought, *nothing could be worse than that, but just as bad* was how she'd fallen for his lies, and all the cheap tricks that cheaters play. Lately, whenever Polly questioned him about his strange behavior or caught him in a small lie, he'd twist the conversation and act like he was the accuser instead of the accused. "Why are you acting paranoid and suspicious?" he'd complain, insisting he had nothing to hide. And for the most part, Polly had bought his excuses and cover stories. But a nagging intuition had told her things weren't right between them. Still, she resisted playing the jealous wife. She didn't check his laptop or cell phone for texts, or other evidence he might be up to something. And so far, she hadn't lingered in any doorways to eavesdrop on his phone calls.

Back when they were first married, they had made a pact that they would never cheat on each other. On a lazy Sunday morning in bed, Polly had sat astride a naked Christian. "If one of us wants out, then we speak up," she'd said. "We lay it all out and go our separate ways, but no sneaking around. Agreed?"

With his hands cupping her bare breasts, he'd nodded, distracted. "Agreed."

A few weeks back, Polly had reminded Christian of the promise they had made to each other. "We have to be honest and willing to talk about any problems in the marriage."

"I know," he'd said, waving her off. "Nothing's changed. Stop being weird."

That morning, when she'd set out for work, Polly hadn't planned to follow Christian and spy on him. It just so happened that as she was leaving the studio to grab a salad for lunch, she'd noticed his gym bag on her car's back seat. He must have left it there the day before when he'd borrowed the car. His last stop after work was always the gym for a workout, so he'd be needing the bag. She thought about calling his office to let him know she had it, but changed her mind. She'd drop it off in person instead. When she'd pulled up to the office where Christian worked, she'd arrived just in time to see him leave the building, cross the parking lot, and get into his black Jeep. So, she'd followed. *I'll surprise him and we can have lunch together,* she'd thought, realizing right away that she was lying to herself. The forgotten gym bag was just an excuse to check up on him and find a way to confirm her suspicions.

Polly had tailed Christian for a good twenty minutes before he'd pulled up to his destination—a dive bar called the Oasis that was situated in a small strip mall. That's when she first noticed the blonde. She was waiting in the parking lot, and when she saw Christian drive up, she got out of her BMW to greet him. Just a chaste kiss hello. *Could be innocent,* Polly had thought, as she spied on them from her hiding place. The sexy stranger might be a client or a prospect. But then she watched as Christian held the bar door open for her. He looked around to see if anyone was watching them, and Polly's heart sank. There was something in his look that signaled he was up to no good. She had debated following the pair inside but talked herself out of it. *Get a grip. You can't just barge in. What will you say? "Well hi there, Blondie, I'm Christian's wife. What are you up to, looking so tasty on this fine day?"* If this was a legit client meeting, Christian would be furious at her for spying on him. Instead, she'd stayed in her car, anxiously watching and waiting until they came out. Then, she'd witnessed them kiss, a lovers' kiss that confirmed what she had known for months—Christian was cheating on her and lying about it.

Polly pulled into the driveway of the townhouse she and Christian had bought three years earlier and exited her banged-up car. She unlocked the front door and made her way to the kitchen. She spied the chicken she'd left to defrost on the kitchen island and returned it to the fridge. Christian was headed out of town in the morning for business, so as a treat, she had planned to cook him one of his favorite dishes, coq au vin, and serve it with the mid-priced Bordeaux he loved. *Change of plans*, she thought, as she opened the bottle of red and poured herself a glass. Yes to drinking, no to cooking. She wandered upstairs to the bedroom and opened her dresser drawer. Wrapped in tissue paper was the pale blue, lace-trimmed, silk nightie she had bought especially for tonight. She had eyed it just days earlier in a high-end lingerie store in the mall. The sexy underwear had brought back memories of long, sensuous nights with Christian, and how he had always responded to her beauty and seduction. One sultry evening, soon after they had begun dating, Polly had swapped out the T-shirt and boy shorts she typically wore to bed for a silk teddy with matching panties that she'd bought on a whim. Christian's eyes had widened, as he watched her stand in the bedroom's doorway, arm reaching up, while she leaned against the door frame, the other hand placed firmly on her cocked hip. She had curled her black hair and topped off her subtle make-up with a pop of bright pink lipstick. "Hello," she purred, as a tumble of curls fell over one eye. She watched how his body responded. "Hell yeah," he'd said hungrily. "You look like a goddess. Get over here, now."

They'd just started seeing each other and the sex was great, but that night, as Polly tried on her new persona as a glamorous vixen, their love making had hit a new level. She had always loved Hollywood's great sex sirens—Marilyn, of course, Rita Hayworth, Jane Russell, and later, Brigitte Bardot. Much of her passion for dance and musical theater had come from watching Hollywood bombshells perform in unforgettable musicals. Who could resist Marilyn singing *Diamonds Are a Girl's Best Friend?* Or Rita Hayworth shimmying to *Put the Blame on Mame, Boys?* On that night, six years ago, Polly's sexy dress-up, and Christian's response, had unlocked a deep sensuality in her that made her feel feminine, beautiful, and powerful.

As Polly had stood in the mall, studying the blue silk nightie in the store window, she had thought back to that long-ago steamy night, and started fretting about the insecurities that now routinely racked her. *Maybe it's my fault*, she told herself. *Maybe all my suspicions and harping are creating distance and stifling the sex.* She visualized herself in the soft, silky garment that was draped on the mannequin in the display. The deep V-neck and shoestring straps would show off her breasts that were surprisingly round and full against her dancer's otherwise lean body. The hem would graze her crotch and touch the top of her long, toned legs that Christian loved to lift and wrap around him.

Inside the store, Polly had handed the sales assistant her credit card, and left with the pink bag containing the confection of tissue paper and pale blue silk. On the drive home, she had psyched herself up. *Let's see if this can work some magic.*

Now, Polly set her wine glass down on the bedroom dresser. Her lingering doubts and worries about her marriage had crushed her self-confidence. Once hot nights in bed with Christian were growing colder. They still had sex, and he was still hungry for her, but his desire seemed fleeting, and once satisfied, she could see how his thoughts turned elsewhere. Today, in the parking lot, she'd gotten an eyeful of his mistress, so at least she knew now why he was so distracted, and where his thoughts went when he had that distant look on his face.

She took the blue nightie from her dresser drawer and unfolded the sexy garment. Now it only mocked her naive notion that she could fix her marriage with a home-cooked meal and a night of smoldering sex in lacy lingerie. In the mirror, she caught sight of her frowning face and saw early signs of elevens, the two vertical worry lines between her eyes. She thought about the last few months and Christian's guilty behavior. More than once, he'd come home in the early morning hours, claiming business meetings had kept him out late. He kept his phone on him at all times, clearly worried that she might get her hands on it and discover something damning. And he was throwing off a strange energy. Sometimes distant, and then, at other times, almost too affectionate, like he was compensating for something. "Penny for your thoughts," she would say, when she caught him with a far-away look in his eye, but he would brush her off. "Just work stuff."

Instead of acknowledging the signs that her husband was cheating, it had been easier to put the blame on herself and vow to work harder at fixing a marriage she hadn't broken. She smoothed away the frown lines with her finger and talked to her reflection in the mirror. "You're not a kid anymore, Polly. You're coming up on thirty-three. You've given Christian six of your best years. Don't waste any more on what can't be saved." But even as she said this, she was filled with insecurity. On what planet would she ever be able to walk away from Christian Caldwell? Handsome, successful, going places, with the world at his feet. He had captured her heart long ago, and she worried that now, even after he'd broken it, she wouldn't be able to take it back from him. Balling up the nightie, she crushed the soft fabric and crammed it in the drawer.

She took a sip of wine and eyed the time. It was almost four o'clock. Great, she was day drinking. *Well,* she thought, *a girl is entitled to drown her sorrows when she catches her husband groping his side piece, chases after her, and winds up running her new car into a pick-up truck.* She made her way back to the living room and flopped onto the couch. She let the tears come. Christian would be home around 7:00 p.m., giving her about three hours to decide how to handle this debacle. Her instinct was to ready her claws, fly at him, and call him out for the no-good jerk he was, but instinctively she knew this approach wouldn't get her anywhere. As it was, Christian probably had enough wiggle room to mount a credible defense against her accusations. If she confronted him now, he would swear Blondie was a business associate; convince her that it was all just a silly misunderstanding, and she was a paranoid idiot. No, she had to grit her teeth and say nothing, until she could put together an iron-clad case, and confront her cheating husband with so much evidence there was no way he could worm his way out of it.

***

"I'm home." Christian slammed the front door, dropped his keys on the hall table, and sauntered into the family room, tired from his usual strenuous workout. Realizing he'd forgotten his gym bag in Polly's car, he'd made do with the spare gear he kept in his locker at the gym. It was after 7:00 p.m., but there was no welcoming smell of coq au vin cooking. No crusty bread and salad on the dining room table. No Bordeaux opened and ready for pouring in the paper-thin glasses, on the perfect place settings that Polly always arranged for their special dinners. Instead, he found his wife slumped on the couch, still in her dance clothes, next to a half-finished bottle of red wine. He settled into a chair and eyed her. "What gives?"

"I had a bad day and got into a fender bender," Polly mumbled without looking up.

Christian frowned. "How bad is it?" When Polly didn't answer, he stood and made his way to where her car was parked in the driveway to survey the damage. He soon came back inside, looking annoyed. "What happened, Polly?"

"I blew through a stop sign in a parking lot, and a guy in a pick-up truck hit me." There was something in her tone and manner that told him not to push the issue. "I'll take care of it without going through the insurance so it doesn't jack up the premiums," she said, still not making eye contact.

"What does dinner say?" Christian tried to sound cheerful. Polly scowled. "Dinner says there's cold cuts in the fridge, so knock yourself out." She stood up and headed upstairs to run a bath. Christian reached for the abandoned bottle of Bordeaux and poured himself a glass.

***

The next morning, Christian rose early, showered, and dressed. He was headed to Chicago for a four-day tour of the agency's Midwest clients. He grabbed his carefully packed bag that held an immaculately cut Armani suit, assorted shirts, casual wear, and gym clothes. He never missed a workout, even when he was traveling. Christian was a looker and he knew it. Over six feet tall, broad-shouldered, rich brown hair and classically handsome face, with a smile that was wide and captivating. He charmed women and men alike. It's what made him so good at his job in business development at a boutique but high-impact marketing agency. The agency's headquarters were in New York, but Christian worked most days out of the Westchester office, about fifty miles north of Manhattan, and only ten minutes from home.

The star marketing executive was charismatic. Guys didn't seem to mind that their wives and girlfriends fawned over him, because when he shook another man's hand and looked him directly in his eyes, Christian signaled he was all about the bro code. Sure, the ladies loved him, but he was a guy's guy at heart, ride or die. And he had all the guy credentials. He was a gym rat who played soccer on the weekends with his buddies, took winter trips for black-slope skiing, and spent hours on the golf course, forging bonds, talking business, and doing deals. And yeah, he'd been known to arrange bachelor parties for friends, in New York and Vegas, that may or may not have involved strippers. These were nights to remember but never to be spoken about. Bro code.

Morning light streamed through a gap in the drapes, as an awake Polly feigned sleep. She could hear Christian moving about the bedroom with military precision, checking his bag, his phone, his lists. Finally ready to leave, he bent to kiss his wife's nose. "Bye, beautiful. I'll text you when I get there." Polly kept her eyes closed and muttered a reply. A few minutes later, she heard the front door close and the Jeep's engine start. Her cheating husband was headed out of town, and she had only four days to figure out her next move.

CHAPTER 2: AMBITION

After Christian left, Polly lay in bed, thinking about how she was no match for him. The man was a machine, organized, calculating, and always in control. It was what she'd once loved about him. The way he took charge, kept their lives running smoothly, planned his career moves, and climbed the corporate ladder to keep the money and opportunities flowing. But it hadn't always been that way. Polly was twenty-six and Christian thirty-one when they had first met, six years earlier. He had been in a dead-end job at the time, working in sales for his father's building supply company. Back then, it was Polly who had enjoyed a successful career whilst playing cheer leader for a struggling Christian, who complained that as the youngest of three sons working in the business, he wasn't getting the respect, the opportunities, or the money he deserved from his father.

"Polly danced out of the womb," her mom, Annie, had always said about her youngest daughter's burning desire to be a dancer. From the moment she could wiggle her diapered butt in a pink tutu, Polly had begun her dance through life.

"Keep your grades up and you can have as many dance classes as you like," Annie had told her daughter, and Polly had taken her up on it. Ballet, jazz, tap, ballroom, modern, you name it, the aspiring dancer pursued it all. Her family wasn't rich, just solidly middle class, with three kids, a dad who was an electrician, and a mom who was a nurse, but Polly's parents had fed their youngest child's dance habit. Their investment had paid off. The talented dancer won roles throughout school, and later she secured parts in local theater. As she matured, she began taking classes with esteemed teachers, winning spots in supper clubs, revues, even roles in new works from up-and-coming choreographers.

At eighteen, Polly had moved to Manhattan and discovered how tough life could be for a wannabe hoofer in the big city. She gigged as a hostess, a waitress, and a cloakroom attendant to pay for her room in the shoe box apartment she shared with two other dancers on Manhattan's Upper Westside. She worked all the lowly jobs that passionate performers take to eke out a living and follow their star. But Polly had just enough lucky breaks to keep her in the game and stop her from giving up in the face of long odds and grueling competition. Technically, she wasn't the best dancer around, but she was extremely watchable and drew the eye. In any group of dancers, an audience would eventually be drawn to the beautiful girl with the raven hair, long, lovely limbs, and sensuous presence, who danced with so much style and exuberance.

The email awarding her the role of Velma Kelly in the musical *Chicago* had come on Polly's twenty-sixth birthday. She had escaped the city to visit her family for a long weekend of celebration, and the news that she'd won the part was the best gift of all. Twenty-six wasn't old, but for a dancer, it was a reminder that the clock was ticking. The window was closing on the opportunity to break out and avoid getting trapped in the chorus, or stuck as some run-of-the mill dancer, who tap danced and pirouetted from one bit part to another. Polly understood all too well how injuries mount up and the body breaks down. The spirit and stamina needed to take the classes, do the drills, go on auditions, and face the never-ending rejection, finally fails. Then the dancer's short career is over, and the rising star sputters out before it ever has a chance to shine. But that wasn't going to be Polly's fate. She was going to star in the production of *Chicago* that a nearby, regional dance company called StepWorks was mounting. The director was planning a twenty city tour of the US, followed by a hiatus, and then a ten city tour in Europe.

"Mom, I got the part," she'd yelled, as she opened the email and read the good news. Annie came tearing down the stairs of the family's modest, four-bedroomed house, and Polly jumped up to hug her. "I did it! I'm going to Europe. I'm a professional dancer in a major role for a serious company."

That night, Annie cooked a celebratory dinner of chicken cutlets, mashed potatoes, and peas, followed by a store-bought birthday cake. Polly sat at the head of the table, as her brother Mattie, sister Nicki, and her parents, all stood and raised their glasses. "To Velma Kelly," her father, Patrick, toasted. "To Velma Kelly," the rest of the family cheered. Polly took a sip of the cheap champagne and blew out the candles on her cake. "Make a wish," her mom insisted, but in that moment, Polly couldn't think of anything. "I already got my wish," she said, giddy with happiness.

"Here's to not breaking a leg!" Mattie shouted. They all touched their glasses together for a second toast, and nobody stopped to consider that a broken leg isn't the only calamity that can derail a promising career.

Polly threw herself into rehearsing the role of Velma Kelly. The inaugural performance was at a local dinner theater that was home base for the StepWorks Dance Company. From there, they would tour the country, performing at mostly second-string theaters and venues in twenty cities, before returning and doing their two final shows at the theater where they had kicked off the production.

Polly loved being on the road and her time on stage, performing six nights a week to standing ovations. She enjoyed traveling with the company and exploring the American towns they passed through as they grabbed a precious few hours of downtime. She was popular and made friends easily, but the person Polly connected with best, confided in most, and spent the majority of her free time with, was Danelle, a talented and versatile dancer, who played one of "Chicago's" Merry Murderesses. The petite dancer's mother was Puerto Rican, her father African American, and Danelle was a glorious melding of the two. She had copper ringlets, gray-blue eyes, caramel skin, and a dancer's lithe body. Danelle was also a festival of fragrance. Her curls and skin always smelled delicious, and wherever she went, she trailed the intoxicating odor of Black Opium perfume. All the women in the company dabbed on the scent, trying to recreate how it smelled on Danelle, but no go. There was something about the way Danelle's skin and the perfume combined to create a scent that had everyone sniffing the air and proclaiming, "What is that amazing fragrance?"

On the night Polly met Christian Caldwell, she had been in the women's changing room after the show with Danelle and the other dancers. It was the final performance of *Chicago's* US tour, at the dinner theater in Westchester, where they had started out months earlier. And it was only a fluke that Christian happened to catch the last show of the run.

***

To celebrate their parents' wedding anniversary, Christian's brothers had arranged a family night out to see the musical. Dinner theater with a middle-aged crowd was the last place Christian wanted to be on a Saturday night, when he could be in a sports bar, picking up girls, with his friends, he'd told Polly later. But he had settled in to make the most of it, and when the house lights had dimmed, the spotlight had found Polly, looking like an absolute knockout, on the darkened set. "The body on you was amazing, as you performed the bump and grind all over the stage, belting out *All That Jazz*. I had to meet you," he'd confessed to her.

After the show, when he went backstage to find her, he claimed that he almost didn't recognize her without the short Prince Valiant wig, and thought she was even lovelier than he had first realized, once he got an up-close look at her long dark hair, pale skin, green eyes, and long, lean dancer's body. Not to mention, the full breasts he detected through her thin dressing gown as he handed her his business card. Seducing women was Christian Caldwell's superpower, but once in a while, a woman came along who stirred more than sexual longing in him, and Polly Sullivan was one of those women. He had read her name in the program. The role of Velma Kelly was played by Polly Sullivan.

For her part, Polly had marveled at how the handsome intruder had managed to talk his way into the changing room, where half-naked dancers were gossiping as they changed out of their costumes, discussing that evening's performance, and making plans for what was left of the night. With those good looks, this guy can get away with anything, an exhausted Polly had thought, immediately perking up at the sight of her unexpected but exciting visitor. He's so damn appealing. Like Moses parting the Red Sea, Christian had flashed a devastatingly handsome smile, and a small sea of showgirls had opened up a path, so he could stroll up to Polly. He stood over her, tall, virile, and sexually magnetic, as she examined the black embossed printing on his business card: "Christian Caldwell, Head of Sales, Caldwell Brothers Building Supply Company." When she looked up from the card and into his handsome face, his dark brown eyes met her green ones with a smoldering gaze.

"Call me," he ordered her.

"And if I don't?" Polly asked. Her dressing gown had fallen open slightly to reveal a portion of her creamy left breast. He looked right at it, making no effort to hide his desire. He licked his lips as if to suggest his intentions. "If you don't call me," he said, "then I'll just have to come back, and keep on coming back until you do." Christian glanced around the dressing room. "And I am sure these lovely ladies don't want me to keep intruding on their privacy."

"You can *intrude* on my privacy anytime," Polly heard Danelle proclaim from somewhere in the back, and the entire room erupted in laughter. Polly blushed and couldn't help but smile. "Okay get out of here," she said.

"You gonna ring me?" Again there was a commanding note in his voice.

"I'm going to think long and hard about it," Polly replied.

"Long and hard sounds about right." Christian winked and Polly blushed. She turned her back to the sexy intruder and faced the mirror to finish taking off her makeup. He caught her eye in the glass. "You're beautiful," he mouthed silently, then he turned and walked out. After the door closed, there were more peals of laughter from the gaggle of half-dressed dancers.

"Polly if you are not going to call that fine gentleman, could you please hand me his card?" Danelle held out her hand. Her arm was glistening with sweat after her strenuous dancing, and her skin gave off its usual, delicious aroma of Black Opium perfume. Polly laughed and tucked the card in her purse, away from Danelle's clutches. Later, the two best friends grabbed a drink together. "You gonna call that guy, Christian?" Danelle asked.

"I don't know," Polly said, looking into her beer. "I'm too tired to think. I just want to hang out with the family, do my laundry, and catch up on some sleep." The pair of exhausted dancers touched glasses. "To sleep."

Of course, Polly Sullivan did call Christian Caldwell, but she waited until a respectable seventy-two hours had passed and she was well rested and coming down from the strenuous tour schedule. Discovering they lived in adjoining towns, the pair arranged to meet at a deli that was exactly a twenty-minute drive for each of them. Settled in a red vinyl booth, the shiny plastic tabletop between them, they both ordered milkshakes, chocolate for him, vanilla for her. They decided to split an oversized turkey sandwich, as they talked nonstop.

"You were amazing. I couldn't take my eyes off you," Christian gushed, describing for the first time the story he would repeat often, that Polly's performance had transfixed him. He hadn't even wanted to be there that night, he admitted, as they sat opposite each other in the diner, leaning in as close as they could with the table between them. Lucky for him, he had let his brother talk him into attending the show. How else would he have ever known she existed? He didn't hold back. He wanted Polly to know exactly how hard he had fallen for her. Their conversation never halted for a second and hit no awkward pauses, as they flirted and bonded and Christian probed her for her biography. "Not much to tell, really," she confessed. "My life has been all about family and dance, dance, dance. All I ever wanted was a career as a dancer. Now that I have one, I just spend every minute enjoying my good luck and thanking my lucky stars that I'm getting paid for what I love to do."

"No boyfriends?" Christian asked.

"No time for boyfriends," Polly scoffed like her decision not to date was a no-brainer.

"You're not a virgin?" Christian teased.

"Of course not!" Polly grunted in disgust. "There was a guy in high school and a couple of dancers I hooked up with for a while, and plenty of casual dates, but I just don't have enough time and energy left over from dancing to spend on relationships." Christian gave her a sad puppy look and

Polly laughed.

After three hours, their waitress was giving them the evil eye. "I have to close out my station," she said finally with a forced smile, which barely masked she was ready for them to give her a tip and get the hell out.

"Wanna go to a bar?" Christian asked, as they stood at the cash register, while he paid the check.

"Sure." For the first time in months, Polly was free to luxuriate in the company of a handsome man with no place to be, no rehearsal to make, no performance to give.

"Know where Callahan's Bar is?" Christian asked.

"I do."

"Meet you there in ten?"

"Sounds good."

Outside, she got in her mom's beat-up Pathfinder and texted her mother.

Polly- Mom, I'm on a date with the cutest guy. Don't know when I'll be done. Please can I keep the car for the rest of the day? Please!

Mom- Fine, her mom texted back with a grumpy emoji.

At Callahan's Bar, it was Christian's turn to open up more. As he spoke, Polly studied his handsome face, his full mouth, the way he licked his lips when he paused to think of something, or gestured with his hands, somehow curling his long sim fingers in the air, as he talked about his past in a way that made the scenes he described come alive. As she watched and listened, mesmerized by Christian's charisma, good looks, and strong sexual appeal, Polly noticed she would momentarily lose track of what he was saying. Instead, as she watched his delicious mouth forming the words of his colorful stories, she thought about how she wanted him to kiss her with that irresistible mouth, caress her with those strong hands, and stroke her in her most intimate places with those expressive fingers. He didn't have a steady girlfriend right now, she heard him say. He was focused on work, but he was frustrated. "Dad wants us three brothers to work in the family business and eventually take it over, but he won't hand over the reins," he complained. "I have plenty of good ideas on how to grow the company and expand the marketing, but Dad's old school, stuck in his ways. He thinks he knows best about all things, at all times."

"So what are you going to do?" Polly asked.

"I'm studying for an MBA online," Christian announced. "When I have that at the end of the summer, I'll try talking to Dad one last time to see if we can get on the same page. If not, I'll look for a well-paying marketing position in a company where I can have a future. New York is a mecca for marketing companies. I have plenty of business experience, winning accounts for the family business, and soon I'll have the academic credentials I need." Looking pleased with himself, he chugged his beer. Polly thought he exuded an air of absolute confidence that she found to be a turn on. *My goodness he is beautiful,* she remarked to herself for the tenth time. But his appeal transcended good looks. Maybe it was pheromones, some kind of animal scent, because Christian's sexual magnetism combined with his good looks was intoxicating. Polly realized she was aroused and the longer she sat with him, the more aroused she became. She needed to get out from under his spell and gather herself.

"Excuse me." Polly stood and headed for the bar's restroom. Once inside, she turned to lock the door and felt someone on the other side push it open. Christian eased himself into the tight space and locked the door behind him. He wasted no time. Pressing his mouth against hers, he slipped his hand inside her shirt to knead her firm breast. "I've been thinking about this for over three days," he said, urgently mashing his lips onto hers. She let out a moan. "Okay," he said, as he unbuttoned her jeans and eased them over her hips, "let's go, pretty lady." He turned her around until she was leaning over the sink with her back to him. Polly didn't recognize herself in the small mirror above the basin she was clutching. Hers was the face of a woman awash in an ecstasy that climaxed as Christian released himself into her. He nuzzled her neck tenderly as she steadied herself against the basin, and then sat on the toilet seat to watch him zip up his pants and wash his hands. "See you out there," he said, pushing aside a strand of hair that had escaped from her ponytail.

***

The next morning, when Polly awoke, her mind was filled with thoughts of Christian and what he had done to her in the bathroom at Callahan's. If one of her girlfriends had confessed to doing it on a first date in a public restroom, Polly knew she'd probably be all judgey about it. Hurried sex in the bathroom of a bar with a guy you just met sounded so sordid, but the love making with Christian hadn't felt at all seedy or questionable. Even though it was rushed, it had been incredible. For as long as she could remember, she had been obsessed with one thing—dance, but now this guy comes along who is a force of nature and takes over her thoughts. Polly sat down to breakfast, as Annie served her scrambled eggs and toast. "How was your date?"

"It was amazing," Polly said, her eyes wide and shining, with a look of wonder that Annie only ever saw cross her daughter's face when she was talking about her singular passion—dance. This morning, it seemed a lengthy date with some momentous heartthrob, whom Polly had just met, and Annie knew next to nothing about, was bringing that same rapturous gaze to Polly's face. For some reason, this combined with her mother's intuition, sent a slight tingle of concern down Annie's spine.

Until the European leg of the *Chicago* tour kicked off in three months' time, Polly was free, aside from a light rehearsal schedule. She spent every minute she could with Christian. When he wasn't working, the besotted lovers were together. They ate, drank, watched movies, took walks, and enjoyed insanely good sex whenever and wherever possible. One night, as she dressed for another date with Christian in one of the flimsy tops, no bra, that he favored, she studied herself in the mirror. "How come I never knew sex could be this good?" she asked her reflection.

Later, as they talked over drinks at Callahan's, Christian fixed her with the alluring look he always used when he wanted something. "Do you have to go to Europe?"

"Yes, I have to go," Polly said, a little annoyed at such a ridiculous question. "This is what I've worked for my whole life. Touring Europe in a leading role is a dream come true for me."

"I know, lovely." Christian trailed his fingers along Polly's bare arm, brown as a berry, now that they spent long afternoons sunbathing and drinking beers on a nearby beach that bordered the Long Island Sound. "It's just that I don't know how I can manage without you. I get my MBA this summer and then it's all about leaving the family business and starting a career that can really go somewhere. I want to be able to give us a good life, you know."

Give us a good life? Is he talking marriage? Polly wondered. She knew they were serious. They'd been inseparable for weeks, but she hadn't expected this turn. He was hinting at a long-term, committed relationship, and she felt a flush of pleasure.

"I'm sorry, twinkle toes." Christian kissed her. "No pressure. It's just that when you're around, I feel like anything is possible, like I can conquer the world. I don't want to get in your way. I think we can work it out."

Polly felt a pang of worry. *Think? Did he just say he "thinks" we can work it out? Is he telling me that if I leave for Europe, he's not sure our relationship will last?* She didn't press him, afraid his answer might threaten her happiness. Instead, she stroked his arm and tried to reassure him and herself. "I'll only be gone for six months. I *know* we can make it work." But Christian didn't answer. He just shrugged and turned his

attention to the basketball game on the big screen TV above
the bar.

CHAPTER 3: DANCE

After a night of tossing and turning, and torturing herself with thoughts of Christian's cheating, Polly got up early and made her way to work. She walked into the Beat It Dance Studio that she ran with her partner, Maria. She switched on the lights in the largest of the studio's three rooms. The front wall was mirrored, and two side walls were fitted with practice bars, where Polly put eager young ballerinas through their paces. She had a busy schedule lined up with three private lessons and two classes. Two of the privates were with couples who were learning how to perform a show-stopping first dance for their wedding reception. The third private was with a retired couple. Joan and Colin had taken up dancing as one of the ways, along with golf, travel, and college courses, to avoid stagnating, now that their careers were over and their kids were out of the house. She also had two group classes, teaching beginner and intermediate Argentine Tango. Sensuous and passionate, the tango was a favorite of Polly's. As a lead-follow dance with no set chorography, it demands the woman listen carefully with her whole body to understand where her partner wishes her to go, while he designs the perfect frame for the beautiful picture her movements create. Polly loved the tango's drama, black and red costumes, the strong male and female role-play, the aching beauty of the music, and the tango abrazo cercano, the close embrace.

She had taught Christian a simple tango that they had performed on their wedding day. Part way through the reception, she had changed out of her white, mermaid wedding gown into a silky, hip-hugging, red dress with a thigh-high slit that showed off her long legs in fishnet stockings. After applying a coat of intense red lipstick, she had taken to the floor with her brand new husband, and their tango had been a triumph that had their guests cheering and applauding. *I have love, dance, and the beginning of a beautiful life with a man I adore,* she'd thought to herself that evening, as Christian wrapped her in his arms and lifted her off her feet.

"You are incredible. Are you really mine?" he'd whispered in her ear.

"All yours forever and ever," she'd whispered back.

Now, with the studio all to herself before her first lesson of the day, Polly brought up the music on her play list and began her warmup, slowly rotating her hips in a move called the mess about. The first song to blast through the speakers was one she seldom listened to anymore, because it summoned too many happy memories mixed with painful regrets. Today, however, Velma Kelly's big opening number from *Chicago*, was a song Polly knew would strengthen her resolve. She began to sing along…*Come on babe, why don't we paint the town? And all that jazz. I'm gonna rouge my knees and roll my stockings down. And all that jazz…*As she sang, the dancer checked her form in the mirror. She could remember every step from each of the musical's iconic dance routines. She performed all of them, one after another in quick succession. When she was done, sweaty and spent, she toweled off and drank a bottle of water, thinking back on that magical time when she'd toured with StepWorks. The camaraderie with her fellow dancers, the crowd's thunderous applause after a particularly stand-out performance, and the aching muscles afterward. But most of all, Polly remembered the joy that being a professional dancer brought into her life. She walked around the rehearsal room, her steps echoing in the empty space. Why had she allowed Christian to control her life? To dictate her choices and coax her away from the dance world she so loved, until all her previous joy had leaked out, like water draining from a cracked bucket?

***

At 10:00 a.m., her students Darren and Jodie arrived. For their wedding dance, they had picked the song, "I've Had the Time of My Life" from the movie *Dirty Dancing.* Jodie's mom had died suddenly when her daughter was only fifteen and *Dirty Dancing* had been her favorite movie. In part, the young couple meant for the song and their dance to be a tribute to the mother who couldn't be there for her daughter's special day. Their planned performance was ambitious. They wanted to replicate, as closely as possible, the final dance routine by the characters "Baby" and "Johnny," played by Jennifer Gray and Patrick Swayze, that closed the movie. This included the daring and dangerous lift at the very end, which Polly was trying to modify and tone down for their routine. A bride with a broken neck was not an outcome anybody wanted at a wedding reception.

The couple was making progress and Polly threw herself into coaching them. *These two are going to make it,* she thought, as she watched them giggle and stumble through their choreographed moves. *They really trust each other.* Trust. Now there was a big word. Had Polly ever really trusted Christian? She thought she had. He had taken care of her in so many ways, and yet there was something unknowable about him. The way he enjoyed secret looks and smiles with the men and women who moved in and out of his world. Almost as if he compartmentalized his life. Everyone who knew him, including his wife, knew a different version of him.

***

At 4:00 p.m., with all her classes done for the day, Polly tidied her ponytail in the mirror, grabbed her backpack, and turned off the lights. The full schedule of teaching and dancing had worn her out. But, it had been a welcome distraction from fretting about Christian, his cheating, and the thorny question of how she should handle matters going forward. On her way out of the studio, Polly stopped and peeked into room number two where Maria was working with a couple, probably on a wedding routine. Choreographing wedding or engagement dances was a sizeable and profitable piece of the studio's business. Polly and Maria had set up Beat It Dance Studio over four years ago, and it had grown into a thriving business that provided a decent living for both of them. TV dance competitions had fueled a wave of interest in all things dance, and it now seemed like every bride wanted to put on a show-stopping routine at her wedding. Gone were the days when a couple might settle for shuffling around the dance floor, while a third-rate wedding singer mangled their favorite love song. Today's bride was eager to master a romantic and thrilling dance performance. She wanted to wow her guests and capture the peak experience on video so she could relive it long after her big day had come and gone.

In room number two, The Four Seasons' "Oh What a Night" was blaring through the speaker. Polly caught sight of a playful couple who were cracking up as Maria tried to teach them the steps to the Hustle. The girl was petite with wispy blonde hair, tied on both sides of her head in bunches. She wore harem pants and a halter top. Her partner towered over her, and as he spun the girl around, Polly saw his face. She gasped. It was Marcus, the guy whose pick-up she'd hit. He was laughing hard as the girl stumbled and collapsed into his arms. She slid to the floor as he flopped down beside her. "Guys, please. You've got to take this seriously," Maria scolded. Peering through the window, Polly could see her partner's frustration with the pair, but she quickly ducked so Marcus could not see her. She noticed her heart was racing a little at the sight of him. In between worrying about the rotten state of her marriage, she had allowed herself to think about the attractive pick-up driver that fate had put on a collision course with her. But here he was, dancing with his girl, maybe even planning a wedding, all while he was trying to slide into her DMs. Polly eyed the young woman's bunches. *He likes 'em young,* she thought. *Fresh and without baggage. Yeah, well that's certainly not me.*

Reluctant to take in the spectacle any longer, Polly hurried down the hall toward the exit, away from Marcus and the strange combination of feelings she realized he aroused in her—attraction mixed with caution and distrust, and a thrill of unbidden excitement she couldn't deny. As she opened the door to exit the building, a young guy, dressed for business and carrying a backpack, sprinted toward the door. Polly held it open for him, and he offered a hasty "Thank you" as he dashed past her, headed for room two. *Don't know why you're rushing,* Polly thought. Maria's session with the couple of goof-offs wouldn't be finished for at least another forty-five minutes.

In the parking lot, she gave her crumpled fender the once over. She'd have to take care of it soon. Driving around with a broken headlight was begging for a ticket from the cops. She got in the Subaru and started the engine, still thinking about Marcus. His text right after their accident to suggest his friend's body shop was probably just a pretext to hit on her. Had he noticed her wedding band? If so, did he even care that she was married? He looked to be in a serious relationship, maybe even learning a dance for his wedding day. Did his future wife know he liked to play Sir Galahad to damsels in distress? Polly thought about Christian. How often did he hit on women? Probably every chance he got. And who could resist him? She turned on the radio to distract herself from her disturbing thoughts and then quickly turned it off. Two words kept playing in her mind—Black Opium.

"Siri, call Danelle," she instructed her phone. It rang three times before Danelle picked up. "Danelle, it's Polly." There was a long silence before her former friend spoke. "Long time no hear."

"I know," Polly said sheepishly. She was very aware their relationship had cooled as soon as she'd tied the knot with Christian. Danelle had been hurt that she, supposedly one of the bride's closest friends, had not been invited to the wedding. "I want to come and see you, Danelle," Polly said. Another long silence.

"Okay, when?" Danelle asked, a note of indifference in her voice.

"Tomorrow," Polly replied, relieved that her call to Danelle had broken the ice and opened up communication with her estranged friend.

CHAPTER 4: MARCUS

When Marcus saw Rob come through the rehearsal room door, he stood up and helped Sheri to her feet. "She's all yours," he said, bumping fists with his friend.

"The meeting ended sooner than I thought, so I got out early," Rob said. "Thanks for standing in for me, man." Then, he waved Marcus off, changed out of his work shoes into sneakers, and stood next to his fiancée, ready to master the Hustle.

Out in the parking lot, Marcus climbed into his pick-up and headed toward the Oasis. Once there, he made his way to the office in back to take care of the paperwork that was piling up on his desk. The bar manager sat at his desk and thought about his phone call earlier in the day, with his kid brother. Dawson had been agitated. "Dad is not doing great. He's not recovering from the last operation as well as we'd hoped, and he wants you to come to Kentucky."

"If Dad wants to see me, he can call and ask me himself, not use an errand boy to deliver his messages," Marcus snapped, surprised at how harsh he sounded. His younger brother was a good guy. At twenty-five years old, he was ten years younger than Marcus, and hadn't learned how to say no to their overbearing father.

"Come on, Marcus," Dawson argued. "You know Dad is proud. It's not right to make him grovel, especially when he's been so sick. He's pretty frail these days, and who knows how long it's going to be before he can get his head back into the business. Or if he ever will."

"I'm not asking him to grovel, Dawson." Marcus toned down his annoyance. "I'm just saying if he wants me to come for a meeting in Kentucky, he should call me himself." Marcus knew hell would have to freeze over before Jock Bell III would call him, his eldest son, ten years after he had abandoned the family business for a life in New York.

"If Dad calls will you come?" Dawson asked. Marcus could hear the desperation in his brother's tone. It was his go-to when playing his usual role of peacemaker. Ever since he was a little kid, Dawson had hated conflict. He loved his family—his mom, his dad, and most of all, Marcus, the big brother he looked up to and adored.

"I don't know, Dawson." Marcus' tone was much gentler now. "Look, don't fret over this. Dad is tough. He's going to be fine.

But I want you guys to work out your differences." Dawson sounded plaintive. "Dad could have died if the doctors hadn't caught the cancer in time. No argument is worth breaking family bonds. I know you love the farm. I think you should be here. I want you to be here. I miss you."

"I thought he cut me out of the will?" Marcus's voice was heavy with sarcasm.

"You know that was just anger talking," Dawson argued. "Dad has always wanted you and me to take over the business, and that was his deal with Mom. He swore to it."

"Damn it, Dawson," Marcus said. "I am a thirty-five-year-old man with my own life, my own plans. Jock Bell doesn't get to dictate where and how I work like I'm some hired hand." Realizing Dawson was at a loss for what to say, Marcus reassured him. "Listen, don't fret this, bro. Everything is gonna work out fine, okay?"

"Okay." Dawson sounded dejected.

"I love you, buddy."

"Love you, too." Dawson hung up.

Remembering the call, and feeling annoyed with himself for being so rough with his kid brother, Marcus slapped his hand on his desk, sending a pile of liquor invoices flying. They landed in a scattered mess on the floor. *No one*, he thought, could vex his spirit like his father. He looked at the photo on the wall above the desk. It had been taken fifteen years back. Seemed like a lifetime ago. In it, Marcus could be seen at the tender age of twenty, with his arm around a ten-year-old Dawson. On the other side of his kid brother was their father, Jock Bell III. The three of them were sitting on the white wooden paddock fencing at the family's Turner-Bell Estate in Kentucky's Bluegrass Region. If he closed his eyes, he could recall the day. He pictured the blue sky, and the smell of freshly cut grass. The sheen on a horse's coat after a gallop around the paddock. The stable noises, as farm hands fed, groomed, and moved the horses in and out of their stalls for daily exercise and training. To Marcus, the horse farm was perfection, a magical place, a world he had been born into and loved with every fiber of his being.

Until he turned twenty-five. Marcus Bell had happily embraced his birthright as a fourth-generation Kentucky horse breeder, convinced that he would never leave Turner-Bell Estate, or set foot outside of Kentucky, for anything other than a necessary business trip or brief vacation. But here he was, running a dive bar in a strip mall, fifty miles outside New York City. How much further from breeding racehorses could he get? He studied his father in the photograph. It was all there, Jock's rugged strength, his love of the land and the horses he raised, and his obvious pride in the two sons he knew with certainty would follow in his footsteps. His father had once been Marcus's hero, a man he looked up to, but not anymore. For all his strength and rugged character, Jock Bell had a cruel streak that had caused his family untold pain.

Leaving the estate had felt like an amputation to Marcus, but he was sure he could never go back, not as long as Jock was alive. When he first left home, the displaced Kentucky native had made his way up and down the Eastern Seaboard, scoring jobs as a bar back or bartender in restaurants and bars in the Carolinas, Pennsylvania, New Jersey, and New York City. His goal was simple—get as far away as possible from Kentucky, Turner-Bell Estate, and Jock Bell III.

Jock had been equally adamant that his eldest son should come home and fulfill his responsibilities. When Marcus refused, his father had threatened to write him out of his will and cut him off from the millions of dollars he was set to inherit. The prodigal son didn't care. None of the tactics Jock used to lure him back worked. Now the old man was playing the sympathy card and deploying Dawson to deliver it. Of course, Marcus had been alarmed to learn about his father's cancer diagnosis, but he'd made enough calls back home to get the straight skinny on Jock's condition. The word was that while his old man had been pretty sick and undergone a few serious surgeries, he was on the road to recovery, even though he'd never be able to work as hard and at the same pace as before.

Hundreds of miles separated them, but across the distance, Marcus could pick up Jock's agitation. He knew the older man had glimpsed his own mortality, felt his body turn on him, experienced his strength lessening. All of which had left the headstrong father frantic to engineer his son's return.

When Marcus's parents married, their families had combined their neighboring farms and merged their interests. "One day, you boys will own this place," Jock would tell his sons, as the three of them strolled the rolling pastures of the sprawling Turner-Bell Estate. While Dawson rode on Jock's shoulders, Marcus strode alongside them, listening to his father's deep, rich Kentucky twang, as he repeated his oft-told stories about how his own father had gone from being a lowly farmhand to owning a stake in the magnificent property they now walked.

Marcus analyzed the photo and the slight smile that played across his old man's lips. Jock appeared to be master of all he surveyed. He had secured the Bell dynasty and mapped out his sons' futures perfectly, or so he'd thought. But in a dive bar in New York state, surrounded by acres of concrete instead of fenced-in pastures, his oldest son thought otherwise. "You screwed up, Dad," Marcus muttered. "You screwed up big time."

PENELOPE HOLT

CHAPTER 5: DANELLE

Polly got in her car and headed north. Maria was covering for her at the studio. The two partners often balanced the studio's workload by teaching each other's classes, while splitting costs and responsibilities for running and marketing the school. They made decent money, working on the periphery of the dance world as instructors, but copping to being a dance teacher made Polly wince. She'd always known, like many dancers before her, that as her career wound down, she'd likely turn to teaching. She just hadn't expected it to happen so fast and interrupt what had been a career full of promise.

Christian's pressure campaign to push Polly out of performing had been slow but relentless. Whenever she faced the choice of moving forward in her career or staying put, Christian had persuaded her to stay put. He convinced her to forego opportunities, avoid rejection, and relax her commitment to grueling rehearsals and auditions. He had methodically undermined her ambition, subtly distancing her from her once strong relationships in the dance community. He'd coaxed her out of taking any jobs that might interfere with their home life and disrupt their routines as a couple. And he had done it in a way that made

Polly feel like all his decisions were her own. He convinced her that she, not him, was the one scuttling her plans of being a professional dancer, the dream she'd chased since she was a little girl.

When she first met Christian, Polly had learned fast that there was one thing she hungered for more than dance, and his name was Christian Caldwell. Thinking about it now, she was shocked to realize just how much of herself she'd been willing to give up to be with this intoxicating man, who had a masterplan to deliver la dolce vita—the sweet life. Only life never was as sweet as Christian had promised it would be.

Following the GPS, Polly navigated backroads until she reached the small Connecticut town that Danelle had escaped to three years ago, when she'd married Lou and given birth to their son, Louis Junior. *The baby must be two,* Polly thought, trying to calculate the time and distance that now separated two friends who had not only been inseparable soul sisters but dancing queens. Pulling up to the cute yellow house with black shutters, she saw a charming New England cottage. It even had a white picket fence and narrow stone path leading to the front door, where Danelle appeared before Polly had a chance to knock. Her friend looked the same as always, with her petite dancer's frame, the wild curls, gorgeous caramel skin, and the scent of Black Opium wafting around her. She opened the door wide in welcome, and despite the ill feeling that had suddenly bloomed and ended their friendship years earlier, Polly actually sensed somewhere deep down that Danelle might be pleased to see her. "Come in," she said. "I just got Louis down for his nap."

Polly stepped inside. "Aw, I was hoping to meet him," she said, but Danelle ignored her attempt at warmth.

"Want some water? Coffee? Juice?" Danelle rattled off the beverage choices but Polly declined.

Danelle sat on a low couch and gestured to a wicker chair. "Sit." Polly looked around. The place was classic

Danelle. It might have looked like a country cottage from the outside, but inside it was artsy and boho, with brightly colored pillows, rugs, and textiles, accented with plants, wicker, and woven hemp. The home was warm and colorful like its owner.

"Why are you here, Polly?" Danelle asked, offering no small talk to warm up the slightly chilly atmosphere.

"Straight to the point, huh?" Polly replied with a nervous grin.

"I don't see any reason to sugarcoat things. It's not like we're friends anymore." Danelle couldn't resist the jab.

"Ouch." Polly winced. "I suppose I deserve that. I'm sorry, Danelle. I made a mistake agreeing to let Christian exclude you from our wedding. I've made a lot of mistakes, but maybe I'm not the only one." It was Polly's turn to fix her hostess with a cool expression. Danelle shifted in her seat.

"You know," Polly went on, "I always thought Christian didn't want you at the wedding because he was angry at you for insisting I stay in Europe and not abandon the tour, when he was adamant that I leave Paris and go home with him. He made it clear to me that since you tried, in his view, to sabotage our relationship, you weren't welcome at the wedding. I explained you were just trying to support your friend in the best way you knew how. You knew how much the tour meant to me. You were convinced that my ankle injury would heal, and that I should stay and see it through to the end."

Polly paused and looked at Danelle who remained silent. "But we both know the real reason Christian didn't want you to come to our wedding. It was because you and he slept together in Paris. My fiancé and my best friend went behind my back and had sex. Then both of you launched the charade of acting like you were looking out for me, when you were actually screwing me, or each other, I should say."

"Did Christian tell you we slept together?" Danelle asked calmly.

"Of course not," Polly scoffed. "Christian doesn't confess, because Christian is too clever to get caught—most of the time."

Danelle eyed her coolly. "Then how do you know? It happened a long time ago, and no one else knows about it." Polly went quiet. On the drive up, she had hoped against hope that Danelle would deny the accusation and launch a strong defense, like Christian always did, whenever she accused him of wrongdoing he knew she couldn't prove. She couldn't really be certain that Christian and Danelle had betrayed her unless one of them confessed. The faintest suspicion they'd had an affair had always just laid there at the back of Polly's mind where she ignored it. She'd finally allowed it to blossom in the middle of the night, right after she'd caught Christian kissing the blonde outside the Oasis. What had always seemed unthinkable, Christian cheating on Polly with her best friend, suddenly appeared not only possible but likely.

Danelle didn't say anything, so Polly went on. "The day after Christian flew in to see me in Paris and propose, I was still laid up with my busted ankle in the hotel room. He was restless and said he wanted to go for a walk and get some air, maybe grab a coffee. When he came back a couple of hours later, he smelled of you, of Black Opium, absolutely unmistakable. The scent clung to him. I asked if he had run into you. I don't know why he lied and said no. He could have easily said he saw you in the lobby and invited you along for a walk, but he denied even seeing you, and yet your smell was all over him." Polly saw Danelle staring at her with an expression that was halfway between defiance and embarrassment. "I didn't want to believe it, obviously," she went on. "I was madly in love with him. We'd literally just gotten engaged the day before. There was no way I thought he'd cheat on me with anyone and definitely not with you. You were my best friend, the person I trusted most."

Danelle lowered her eyes. "I'm sorry, Polly. I never intended for it to happen," she said quietly.

"So what did happen?" Polly asked calmly. "Even if we're not friends anymore, I'd like to think that woman to woman, you still have enough respect for me to tell me the truth."

Danelle nodded and began in a slow, steady voice. "That day in Paris, Christian and I arranged to go out for coffee to talk. I didn't tell you because I planned to give him a good telling-off and didn't want to upset you. You were vulnerable and anxious. An ankle injury like you had can be career ending, and I knew your mind was full of worry about the future. I saw how Christian was pressuring you to quit the tour permanently and go back to the states, enticing you with an engagement ring. He was manipulating you to get his way." Danelle sensed her old friend knew she was telling the truth.

"Go on," Polly said.

"I met Christian in the hotel lobby. We went to a small bistro around the corner. We got into a heated argument about the best way to handle your injury and the tour. After a while, he put on this act, like he was taking my concerns to heart. 'You're right,' he said. 'Maybe I am being unfair to Polly.' He talked about how much he loved and missed you while you were gone. How he just wanted what was best for you. He thanked me for being a good friend, and said he'd think seriously about what I'd said. I was pleased. Mission accomplished. I'd gotten him to back off. We paid the check and got ready to leave." Danelle fell silent.

"And?" Polly prompted her.

"I excused myself and went to the bathroom. I didn't realize Christian was behind me. He pushed his way inside." Danelle hesitated, and Polly could feel her insides starting to churn. She gritted her teeth.

"What happened?" she asked, although she already knew.

"We had sex in the bathroom. I didn't want to. It happened so fast. You know I always thought Christian was a handsome guy. He's a flirt and irresistible to almost every

45

woman who sets eyes on him, but I never ever planned to do that, Polly. I swear."

Polly stopped paying attention to Danelle's words. She was thinking back to her first date with Christian in Callahan's Bar. How he had followed her to the bathroom, caught her off guard, and overwhelmed her with his sexual magnetism. Feelings of excitement, desire, and the thrill of clandestine sex. She didn't want to forgive Danelle or cut her any slack, but she understood the element of surprise, how forceful Christian could be, how expert his lovemaking was. She could imagine the tight space of the bathroom and Danelle's confusion. Wanting to refuse but getting aroused as Christian touched her in ways that made it impossible to say no.

Polly had always known Danelle had the hots for Christian, from the first time they met him, when he'd burst into the changing room and Danelle made the crack that he could "intrude" on her anytime. She'd been pretty certain though that Danelle would never act on her crush. She saw now how Christian's calculation had been next-level clever. Once he recognized that Danelle's interference was threatening his relationship, he'd effectively side-lined her by having sex with her. He created a guilty secret that hung over Danelle, kept her quiet, and made it easy for him to push her out of his fiancée's life. And, as an added bonus, he'd no doubt enjoyed his tumble with the young beauty in a Parisian bistro. Hurried sex in a public place could be a big turn-on, and Polly had always thought that this particular seduction was something Christian reserved solely for her. Turns out it was just a cheap stunt in his repertoire that he employed as needed. She closed her eyes tight to block out feelings of hurt and betrayal. She imagined that everyone was laughing at her, or worse, pitying her.

"I'm sorry, Polly," Danelle said. "I never planned it. I felt awful. I wouldn't hurt you for the world."

There it was. There was the pity. Polly knew her friend was sincere, but in her misery, she wanted to punish her.

She looked into Danelle' eyes and saw her pain. *It's cowardly to blame her*, she thought, when Christian engineered the entire mess. Yes, Danelle could have pushed him off and run out of that bathroom in Paris, but Polly knew how hard it was to resist the one-man wrecking ball that was her husband once he was determined to get his way. Hadn't he been leading her around by the nose since the first day she'd met him? Christian's fulltime job at home and at work was to manipulate the people in his life until he got exactly what he was after. She squashed the urge to relieve her hurt by lashing out at her old friend. "I get it, Danelle," she said finally. "I don't like it but I get it."

"I was going to tell you." Danelle's tone was gentle now. "But I was ashamed. I knew it would never happen again, and I just wanted to close the book and forget it. I thought you would rehab your ankle and rejoin the tour. I was shocked when you never came back and married Christian after only six months. I wanted to come to the wedding to show that I supported you in whatever decision you made. It hurt when you shut me out. I figured Christian had been in your ear, poisoning the well, separating you from the people and the things you loved. But hey," Danelle held up both hands, "none of my business. It's your life."

For the first time, Polly saw herself through the eyes of her family and friends. How weak she must look to them. She had abandoned the European tour early because of a routine injury that she could have worked through with enough determination and care. But with Christian continually stoking her fears, she'd been afraid of failing and making a fool of herself. Her family had encouraged her to conquer her doubts and soldier on, but Danelle had guessed right. It was Christian who had her ear. "You need to fully recover," he'd argued. "There'll be other tours after we're married." He had known exactly what he was doing when he brought an engagement ring with him to Paris, knelt before her, and proposed in her hotel room, while she sat with her swollen ankle propped up on a pillow. She now had a bitter realization. I *tossed aside my career for a two-carat, cushion-cut solitaire diamond engagement ring, and a boatload of empty promises.* Christian's proposal in the city of lights, the city of love, had overwhelmed her. In that moment, above all else, she had wanted to marry him. She would have done anything for him, given up every dream, thrown away every cherished ambition, and he knew it.

Back in the US, she had needed support, but Christian only undermined her further. There was no encouragement to get back out there, like thousands of injured dancers before her had done. Instead, he urged caution and playing it safe. "Lean on me," he'd said. "Don't worry about the future. I'm gonna make a great life for us."

Polly had believed she could have the two things she most wanted; marriage and a dance career. With any other man that might have been the case, but not with Christian. Her career was just an inconvenience to him. If he was with a woman, then that woman should be there for him at all times, otherwise, what was the point? Polly existed for his pleasure, and he was not interested in making any sacrifices to support her ambitions.

From upstairs, came the sound of Louis Junior crying. Danelle excused herself and went to bring the adorable toddler downstairs. Polly reached out to touch the small child's hand, but he pressed his face into his mother's shirt. "He's cranky," Danelle apologized. On the wall, Polly glimpsed a row of black and white framed photos of Danelle executing various dance moves. A grand jeté in one. In another, her stockinged leg hung seductively over a practice bar. A third captured a dramatic tango pose. "You still dancing?" Polly asked. Danelle hitched the baby up on her hip and smiled, relieved that the tough conversation she'd always known was coming was finally over. "I'm a part-time yoga teacher if you can believe it. How about you?"

"I'm teaching dance. I have a partner in a small studio close to home. We do okay." Polly felt more bitterness wash over her. Teaching was the consolation prize, a compromise she'd never wanted to make. But being a dance instructor kept the peace because it kept her at home, the way Christian liked it. And by teaching, she at least experienced an echo of what had once driven her—the joy of dance, of movement, music, self-expression, and pushing the body past its limits.

She looked at Louis, who was peeking out from the safety of his mother's arms. Christian had decided he didn't want to consider having children until Polly was thirty-five and he was forty, a good age for a man. Of course, Polly had swallowed the idea like it was her own. "I don't want to think about kids until I'm thirty-five," she would argue whenever Annie pressed her about motherhood now that she'd abandoned performing. "You mean Christian doesn't want children until you're thirty-five...or older?" her mom would challenge. She had her son-in-law's number. She'd seen through him the first time she laid eyes on him, when Polly had brought him for Sunday lunch to meet her family.

"I should be going." Polly gestured toward the door, and Danelle leaned forward unexpectedly to kiss her friend's cheek. "I'm glad you came, Polly. I miss you. I don't know if we can ever be friends again, but I would like it if we could." Polly smiled. If she acted on her plan to leave Christian, she would be needing all the support she could get. "I think we can manage that," she said. "Bye, bye, Louis Junior." She gave a small wave to the toddler who rewarded her with a shy smile. The tension between the women had melted, and it seemed the small hope of a reclaimed friendship and a fresh start might be taking root. As Polly turned to go, Danelle stopped her. "Polly, if you're facing up to hard truths, you might want to consider I might not be the only one."

"Sorry?" Polly said, confusion furrowing her brow.

"I'm probably not Christian's only indiscretion," Danelle stated. Polly nodded. If Christian had cheated with her best friend on the day after he proposed marriage, it stood to reason that in the six years since there would be a long trail of "indiscretions." Danelle had been the first and Blondie was the latest. How many more were in between? Did she even want to know? "You thinking of anyone in particular?" she asked Danelle.

"I heard some stuff," Danelle said awkwardly. "Shouldn't be too hard to figure out." Polly nodded and headed for her car. Once in the driver's seat, she could feel her cheeks blazing with humiliation. *Of course*, she thought, everyone she knew had probably "heard some stuff" about Christian, his women, and his poor, clueless wife. She wanted to cry but stopped herself. *Toughen up, Polly. Playing weak-willed wifey is ruining your life. Time to get a backbone.* She noticed the text notification on her phone.

Marcus- Hi, Polly, it's Marcus. Find a body shop yet?

Polly tossed the phone onto the passenger seat. *Jerk!* The guy was probably only weeks away from getting married, practicing the Hustle with his wife-to-be, and still texting another woman. Men! *The Hustle is the perfect dance for you, Marcus,* she thought, as she started the engine and headed toward home.

CHAPTER 6: THE BAR

Traffic on the ride back from Danelle's was light, and Polly made good time. She decided to swing by the studio to check on Maria. She pulled into the parking lot and parked in her usual spot. She grabbed her phone and noticed a text from Christian. Now on day two of his Midwest charmathon, he'd finally deigned to message her.

Christian- Hi. Sorry I haven't called. Crazy here. Don't forget to book the car in for repairs.

What a complete and absolute asshole. He was hundreds of miles away, and yet the dent in her car was making a dent in the psyche of her control-freak husband. A busted fender was a blot on the pristine image that Christian was always projecting, and she knew he'd keep nagging until she got it fixed.

As she now contemplated Christian's betrayal, Polly felt overwhelmed by an unfamiliar feeling—clarity. Clarity brought anger, and anger motivated her. She had been sleepwalking through the last six years. Under a spell her husband had cast, and one she'd been unable or unwilling to break. *Isn't Prince Charming supposed to wake Sleeping Beauty with his kiss and not put her in a trance,* she thought, recognizing she'd bought into a life dictated by Christian's wants and needs. Then again, how many shows and articles had she seen about unhappy women and their cheating partners? They described their journey to escape the hell they were in, and the moment they acknowledged the depths of betrayal, often with a single memorable phrase; "One morning, I just woke up and realized my husband was…" fill in the blank: "Cheating on me…Leading a double life…Keeping secrets…Controlling everything I did…Making me miserable." Polly understood she wasn't the first to lose herself in a relationship, and she wouldn't be the last, but she did know she wanted this sorry chapter of her life to be well and truly over.

Polly walked into the studio and threw down her bag. The thud as it hit the floor made Maria look up from her phone with a welcoming smile, reminding Polly how her good-natured partner often seemed like sunshine turned into flesh. The tall, lanky brunette of Italian descent had been orphaned at age eight when both parents had been killed in a car wreck on the Bronx River Parkway. Sent to live with her grandmother in the Bronx, Maria had been incapable of learning in school, and was instead a natural dancer. As a girl, she had pranced and whirled her way through a world of adults, who wanted her to read books she couldn't decipher, and solve math problems that were incomprehensible to her. In the face of personal tragedy, academic failure, and adult disapproval, many kids might have withered but not Maria. Polly's partner was one of the "Invincibles," the kind of rare bird that grows up in hardship or trauma, and somehow manages to survive with her spirit intact. Maria had drowned out any heartache, noise, and criticism by cranking up her music and dancing. "As a kid, I felt like nothing could keep me down when I was listening to music and moving my body," Maria had explained to Polly one day in the studio. "When the body moves, the spirit rises," she proclaimed. And with that, the livewire had leapt up and begun blasting "What a Feeling" from the movie *Flashdance*, enacting the high-energy dance that the lead character, Alex, performs for a row of uptight judges.

"You want me to throw a bucket of water on you while you arch your back on the chair?" Polly shouted above the music, offering to make the scene even more realistic. "No, I got it," Maria said, as she dunked a bottle of water on her curls then whipped her head around, shaking the water out of her hair. A perfect imitation of the movie's famous dance sequence.

The two dancers had first met in Manhattan, where they'd moved in the same dance circles, often competing for the same jobs, and sometimes working in the same productions. At a chance meeting four years earlier, they had lingered for three hours over coffee, discussing what was next in their lives. Five years older than Polly, Maria was tired of the grind she faced as a second-string dancer on a competitive circuit. "Bones are getting old and the young 'uns are coming up fast and hard," Maria had lamented, as she bit into a slice of lemon drizzle cake. "I wanna make a move and start teaching, but I'm not sure how to make it happen."

At the time, Polly had been feeling ground down by Christian's carping, every time she accepted a dance gig that took her out of town or had her working on weekends. "I don't know if I want to teach," she'd told Maria during their coffee shop heart-to-heart. "I'm pretty sure I know how to make it happen though." The pair had laughed, and from then on, theirs was destined to be a light, easy partnership. Within a few weeks, their plan to open a small dance school had fallen into place. They leased a space, fitted it out as a studio, and started drumming up business. Maria was over the moon. Christian was smug because his wife had finally seen the light and swapped performing for teaching. Meanwhile, Polly's heart was only half in it, but at least it cut down on the arguments with Christian, even if it caused quite a few with her mother. "You're gonna throw away your dream and all those years of training just to please Christian?" her mom had groused when her daughter broke it to her about the school.

"It's my idea, too, Mom. I'll be using my skills to teach," Polly argued lamely. She knew full well her mom wasn't buying her excuses, and that honestly, in her heart of hearts, neither was she.

Grateful to have the morning's stressful rendezvous with Danelle behind her, Polly now slung an arm around her good-natured comrade and gave her an affectionate squeeze. "Thanks for covering for me again, Maria. You're the best." She eyed the time. "It's three o'clock. You all done for the day?"

"I've got a wedding couple coming in. They're learning the Hustle."

Polly made a face. "Oh, you mean the girl with the bunches and her boyfriend who were rolling around on the floor yesterday?"

"Yeah that was annoying," Maria said. "But that wasn't the boyfriend. He was just a friend who was standing in until the fiancé could get here."

Polly suddenly remembered the young guy who had rushed past her the day before in his hurry to get to Maria's class. "So, the shorter guy in the white shirt is the fiancé, not the tall guy in the black T-shirt?" she asked.

"Yep, the tall guy just gave the girl, Sheri, a ride. I think she works with him in some bar."

Polly was surprised by how much it pleased her to learn that it was not Marcus but his friend who was engaged to the girl with the bunches. "See you tomorrow, Maria." Polly headed for the door, suddenly feeling upbeat despite the crappy week she was having. Maria snapped her fingers. "Oh, I forgot to tell you, Jay from StepWorks rang earlier to see if he could come by and put up flyers. He's launching a revival of *Chicago* and he's getting ready to hold auditions." Polly felt her conscience prick her. Six years ago, she had abandoned Jay's tour in Paris and left the understudy to carry on. She brushed it off. If she wallowed in all her regrets, she'd sink under their weight. "When the body moves, the spirit rises," she called as she skipped out of the studio.

"You said it," Maria shouted after her.

***

In the car, on impulse, Polly dialed Marcus, who picked up on the second ring. "Hey, Marcus, it's Polly, the menace in the Subaru."

"You hit anyone else?" His voice was deep and sexy with just a hint of the South.

"Not today. Not so far, anyway." Polly laughed.

"What can I do for you, ma'am?"

There was definitely more than a touch of the Southern gentleman about this guy. "I do need to get my car into a shop. I'm driving around with a broken headlight," she announced, happy to have an excuse to call the dishy good Samaritan. "Does your offer to help still stand?"

"Definitely. A friend of mine has a shop not far from here. He'll give you a good price."

"Where's here? And what's a good price?"

"Here is the Oasis bar," Marcus said, "in the strip mall where, shall we say, we bumped into one another. And I'm not sure what a good price is, except that it will definitely be a better price than what you can get elsewhere for the same job."

"Sounds good."

"Why don't you swing by the bar. I can give you the body shop info and buy you a drink to calm your nerves," Marcus suggested.

"My nerves don't need calming," Polly fired back.

Marcus laughed. "Well, mine do. Who knows when another pretty lady is going to try and run me off the road."

He thinks I'm a pretty lady. A secret smile crept across

Polly's lips. "Well, like you said, a Subaru is no match for a pick-up truck."

"Lady, where I'm from, it's called either a pick-up or a truck but not both, you understand?" he teased.

He's flirting with me, she thought. "Yes sir, I got it."

"So when should I expect you?" His tone was inviting and firm but not demanding. She checked the time, 3:30 p.m. "I'll be there in thirty minutes."

***

A half-hour later, Polly parked in front of the Oasis bar. How funny, she was returning to the scene of the crime, where, with her own eyes, she'd seen Christian groping his mistress. This time though, instead of just spying on the joint, she got out of her car and ventured inside. Opening the door to the large rectangle room, she found a long main bar, high-top tables, stools, and a back wall with countertop seating. She spotted the young woman with the bunches. Sheri was behind the bar, serving a handful of customers who were either stragglers from lunch, or had wandered in for a quiet drink before the after-work crowd arrived. Marcus was perched on a stool, talking to one of the patrons. He turned around when he heard the door open like he'd been eagerly awaiting her arrival. He stood and met her with a big grin. "Hey Polly, good to see you." Marcus slid his beer down the dark polished wood of the bar, away from other customers, and gestured toward the barstool next to him. "What can I get you?" She nodded toward his almost empty bottle. "I'll take a beer, please."

"Two long necks please, Sheri," Marcus called. The perky bartender grabbed two bottles from the fridge and popped the caps. Polly took one. "Thanks. How's the Hustle working out?" Sheri put her hand on her hip and eyed Marcus. "Did you tell her, big mouth? No one is supposed to know. Although if Rob can't control his flop sweat, we're gonna have to nix nay the whole thing."

"I didn't say anything." Marcus held up both hands and looked at Polly to help bail him out.

"I saw you at the studio yesterday." Polly laughed, electing not to mention she had mistaken Marcus for the groom-to-be. "I run the studio with my partner, Maria."

"You're a dance teacher?" Marcus pointed his bottle at her. She raised and tilted her own bottle in his direction. "I am a dance teacher." When Sheri wandered off to serve a customer at the other end of the bar, Polly caught him staring at her wedding rings. "And you're married?" He sighed, registering the unfortunate fact that had eluded him until now.

"I am married," Polly replied, grasping that in the confusion of the accident, he must not have noticed her rings. She wanted to add "but not for long" and then thought better of it.

"I didn't know that." Marcus took a long draw of his beer. Polly could see he was perplexed, his face reflecting embarrassment mixed with regret. *He's too much of a gentleman to hit on me,* she thought ruefully. *Christian, the man who is supposed to love and cherish me can't keep it in his pants and humiliates me at every turn, but the handsome stranger treats me like a lady, and has too much class to put the moves on a married woman.*

Marcus shuffled awkwardly and set down his beer. "Here, give me your phone and I'll put in the number for the body shop. My pal Reggie is expecting your call." Polly handed over her phone. She noticed a shift in his tone, as he tried to sound all business. *He wants to hide that he's attracted to me. Of course, that's what a good guy does when he realizes a woman is married.* "Thanks." She took back her phone, feeling sad all of a sudden. Amid so many nasty surprises, the attention from Marcus had cheered her up, eased her bruised ego, and given her the small hope that life after Christian might go on. That there were men out there she could trust. She stood up. "I should go."

"No rush, finish your drink." He sounded very matter-of-fact. She sensed he was unwilling to let her leave and ready to act like they were just new acquaintances enjoying a friendly chat to keep her there. "So, how long have you been teaching dance?" he asked, and with that one question, Marcus kicked off a long, easy conversation that flowed, uninterrupted for over an hour.

Polly was reminded of her first date with Christian, in Callahan's Bar, when they had talked nonstop in a marathon session of getting to know each other, but she could tell already Marcus was in a different league than her feckless husband. He wasn't a charmer or an operator. He was sincere, with a quiet strength that invited respect. She told him about her escapades as a dancer. How she had toured America and traveled to Europe but quit because of an injury. "My dance career never really got back off the ground after that," she confessed.

"Why? Because of your injury?"

"No, my ankle healed up quickly. My husband, Christian, didn't like me touring, so I drifted into teaching." Polly could hear the regret in her voice.

"Seems like a shame when you loved performing so much," Marcus sympathized.

"What about you? You weren't born around here." Polly changed the subject, curious to know his story, and unwilling to linger on her many mistakes.

"For that conversation, we need a shot of Kentucky bourbon."

Polly drained the beer she'd been nursing for the last hour. "Why?"

"Because I'm a Kentucky boy by birth, and Kentucky boys drink bourbon." Marcus caught Sheri's eye and signaled for her to bring two shots. Polly noticed again his long, strong fingers he had run along the fender of his truck, feeling for dents. She wondered how it would feel if he caressed her with those hands. She felt a pang of guilt and shoved it aside, annoyed that she still harbored even a shred of loyalty for the dog she was married to. This was the first time since she'd laid eyes on Christian years ago that she'd thought seriously about sex with another man. She had been a one-man woman married to a man who repaid her by screwing piles of women. Why had she ever bought that Christian wanted what she wanted—to be in a trusting, faithful relationship? She knew now that he'd been stepping out on her since day one. Her marriage vows had been sincere. His had been a con. So to hell with their vows.

Marcus caught her faraway look as he handed her a shot of bourbon. "You, okay?" Polly tasted the sharp, smoky liquor, and felt it warm her mouth and throat as she swallowed. "I'm okay."

"No toast?" Marcus raised an eyebrow.

"What would you like to toast to?"

He thought for a while and said, "To recapturing dreams."

"To recapturing dreams." Polly knocked her glass against his. She wanted to lean over and kiss this beautiful newcomer who was making her feel so good after such a bruising few days, but she didn't. "So, what's a Kentucky boy doing so far from home?" she asked.

"My parents are divorced, and I have a younger brother, Dawson. I come from a long line of racehorse breeders. I grew up raising thoroughbreds on the family estate and thought I'd never leave but I did, and here I am, running this place." Marcus stabbed the top of the bar with his finger, as if adding a period to the tight summary of his life story. It was past five and the large room was quickly filling up, as regulars stopped in for their after-work ritual of drinks with friends. A couple of guys were playing pool, and another group was watching a golf match on the big screen TV. Springsteen was playing under the chatter, the laughter, and the clatter of balls coming from the pool table.

Polly studied Marcus's profile. "Why did you leave the horse business if you loved it so much?"

"Why did you stop performing if you loved it so much?" he asked. "Sometimes, it's just a fact that we get blown off course and carried away from doing what we love." He leaned forward to brush away a lock of hair that had fallen across her eyes. Giving in to the urge to be seductive, Polly had deliberately released her long dark hair from its tie and shaken it loose before walking into the bar. "You have beautiful hair. You're a beautiful woman," her companion said. "And now, I should be quiet, because you're a married woman."

"I won't be a married woman for long," she finally admitted, staring into her glass, unwilling to hold back the truth now that she felt completely relaxed with Marcus and could feel the connection between them growing. There, she'd said it out loud, confessed she was done with Christian. After she caught him with the blonde, she'd lain in bed coming to terms with the inevitable. She'd have to leave the marriage. But this hard fact seemed impossible to contemplate, let alone execute. Christian was a force of nature, who went after what he wanted, and only let go when he had no further use for what he'd taken. He might crave variety and pursue other women, but that was just his ego and sex drive talking. Polly knew he still wanted her, was hungry for her, and always had been. Out of everything he owned, he prized Polly the most. Sometimes on a lazy Sunday afternoon, he would petition her with a strange longing in his eyes. "Polly, take off your clothes so I can look at you." Comfortable with nudity, and with a dancer's confidence, she would slowly undress. Christian would stare at her for a long time, turning her this way and that, almost in an act of worship, until he couldn't hold back any longer. Then, using his hands and his mouth, he fell on the body he craved. And she always responded to him with a passion that matched his own, right up until these last few months, when she'd felt another woman's presence swirling around them.

"I've been too forward and offended you," Marcus said, breaking in on her thoughts.

"You haven't offended me. I'm flattered to receive a lovely compliment from a handsome man." She paused and then added, "Beautiful on the inside and out." Now it was his turn to look down, long lashes almost touching his cheeks. Polly stood up. "I should go. Not because I want to, but because I'm afraid of what will happen if I stay." She excused herself and headed for the bathroom. Inside, she locked the door, thinking this was where the similarity between her first date with Christian and today's encounter with Marcus ended. Marcus did not follow her and push his way into the bathroom to dazzle her with sex. She splashed water on her face and tied her hair back in its usual, tidy ponytail.

Returning to the noise and bustle of the busy bar, Polly spied Marcus talking to a blonde. Squinting to get a closer look, it took her a few seconds to realize that the animated flirt chatting up the handsome bar manager was none other than Blondie. With her hair released from its updo, out of her business attire, and dressed down in jeans and a T-shirt, the sexpot looked very different, but it was definitely her—Christian's mistress. Polly contemplated what to do next. *Does she know who I am? Does she even know Christian is married?* He never wore his wedding ring. He had put it in his dresser drawer, right after they were married, with some bullshit excuse about how it was too uncomfortable and made his finger swell. She saw Marcus glance toward the bathroom to look for her and ducked behind a beefy guy who was intent on watching a pool match. Damn! Here she was, hiding from her husband's girlfriend again. Talk about rich! After a minute, Marcus turned away from the flirtatious blonde, signaling an end to their chitchat. Polly noticed Blondie's face fall at the brush off and couldn't help but smile. *You might be my husband's type, but apparently, you don't tempt Marcus,* she thought. Not until her rival was once again huddled in the bar's far corner, talking with her friends, and too distracted to notice her, did Polly rejoin Marcus. She downed the last of her bourbon. "Thanks for the drink."

Marcus stood up with a disappointed look. "Let me see you to your car." He escorted her outside and across the parking lot to the banged-up Subaru. "Let me know how it goes with Reggie at the body shop," he said. "I'm headed out of town for a couple of days and won't be back until Friday evening."

Polly's heart sank. She hated the thought of him leaving town. Giving into the pull of another relationship was madness, and who knew how long it would take to sort her life so she'd be free to date again? Still, knowing Marcus was close by somehow comforted her. "Where are you going?"

"To Kentucky."

"To the estate?"

He looked down. "No. Maybe. I don't know. My mother wants me to come see her. She lives about thirty minutes away from Turner-Bell with her longtime partner, Mac Campbell."

Polly nodded. "I see. Well, safe travels." She paused and tried to sound casual. "Marcus, who was the woman with the blonde hair you were just talking to in the bar?"

"That's Chrissy. She's a regular who lives locally. Do you know her?"

"No, but I think I recognize her from somewhere," Polly hedged. "What's her last name?" Marcus frowned and thought for a while. "Reynolds, I think. Or is it Ryan? No, it's Reynolds, Chrissy Reynolds."

Polly acted nonchalant, even though learning the name of her husband's girlfriend was making her heart race a little. She pressed her car key and the Subaru unlocked with a chirping sound. Marcus opened the door and her breast brushed against his arm as she ducked into the driver's seat, causing an immediate and unmistakable sensation between her legs. The late afternoon was bright and warm. She looked up at him, taking in his bright blue eyes, and delicious mouth. He leaned down and kissed her gently, grazing his lips against hers. She opened her mouth slightly and felt him slip his tongue between her lips and teeth. She met it with her own, and they pressed their mouths together in a kiss that was hungry but somehow still gentle. Polly didn't know how long they stayed that way. Marcus leant down as she sat in the Subaru, her face turned up to meet his, their mouths locked in the thrill of their first passionate contact. Upon emerging from the torrent of pleasure unleashed by the kiss, Polly opened her eyes, and the first thing she saw was Chrissy Reynolds. She was standing outside the bar, drink in hand, staring at them as they unlocked their lips and pulled themselves apart. Marcus followed Polly's worried gaze and saw Chrissy. "You sure you don't know her?" he asked.

Polly shook her head. "Let's just say we've never officially met. Does she have a thing for you because she's giving me the evil eye?"

Marcus looked away, embarrassed. "Maybe. Yes, I think so, but she's not my type."

Polly closed her door, ready to take off, but Marcus tapped on the window so she lowered it. "What now?" he asked.

"I have no idea." She started the engine, and just as he had before, Marcus slapped the car's roof twice to send her off. At the traffic light, Polly glanced up at her rearview mirror, just in time to see Marcus looking her way as he nudged a nosey Chrissy Reynolds back into the bar. *Damn!* she thought. *Two days ago, I was a zombie wife, forcing myself to believe I was happily married. Today, my marriage has stretched to include a blonde mistress, a good-looking stud, and god only knows how many more of Christian's "indiscretions" are waiting in the wings.*

CHAPTER 7: KENTUCKY

Marcus hit the road after dark, figuring if he drove straight through the night, with only a couple of coffee breaks, he could cover the 750 or so miles and get to his mom's Kentucky farm by breakfast. He drove west across Pennsylvania and Ohio, until he reached Cincinnati at around 7:00 a.m., then he headed south toward the stables that his mom and Mac ran, just outside of Georgetown, about seventy miles north of Louisville.

Driving through the Bluegrass Region he loved so much, Marcus lowered the windows and let the fresh morning air fill the truck's cabin. He breathed in the distinct scent of the familiar landscape and let it restore and invigorate him. Home! A collage of happy memories filled his thoughts. He was a boy again, feeding and exercising the horses, mucking out the stables, hiking the trails, and going with his dad to shoot the breeze with their neighbors, other Kentucky horse folk. All of them, like his family, were consumed with the business of breeding, raising, or training racehorses. Millions of dollars were won or lost, family fortunes bolstered or broken, in the fickle pursuit of producing an equine wonder. Top breeders are driven by the dream of raising that once-in-a generation horse that could secure the

Triple Crown of Thoroughbred Racing, by winning three iconic races: The Kentucky Derby, The Preakness, and The Belmont Stakes. Back on his home turf, Marcus let his thoughts turn to the excitement of the horse business. Producing champions and matching a superior horse with a world-class jockey. Best of all, he thought about race day, and the magnificent coupling of horses with riders, as they galloped the course in a crowded field, eating up the track in a feat of skill, courage, and stamina.

Marcus may have deluded himself that running a bar in the congested suburbs of New York's concrete jungle was an okay way to make a living, but now, driving the back roads of his Kentucky home, he accepted that his life in New York was just a tinny replacement for the world he had left behind. A world that could be downhome and folksy but also elegant and genteel. After all, horseracing was the sport of kings. Marcus was perfectly at home in a dimly lit dive bar, but he also knew how to take his place in the Winners' Circle, after a high-stakes horse race brought riches and notoriety for the winners, as well as ruin and hard feelings for the losers. Marcus acknowledged an inescapable truth; It was time to find his way back to his home and his birthright. Not for the money and prestige that were waiting for him there, but because raising horses was in his DNA. For over a hundred years, his family had bet their futures and their money, sometimes down to their last dollar, on the thrilling and often confounding business of raising thoroughbreds.

As he felt the gravitational pull of home, Marcus knew there was only one true thing keeping him up north, and that was the beautiful dancer whose kiss had turned him inside out. Replaying it in his mind as he drove, he became aroused. Shifting around in his seat, he forced himself to admit that this stunning creature was not someone he could leave behind in his rearview mirror. When it came to women, he had a hard and fast rule; leave the married ones alone. But Polly had made it clear her marriage was in a sorry state and she wanted out. Marcus wanted no part of breaking up a relationship, but if Polly did leave her husband, he fancied being there to take his chances and get to know her better.

A little after 8:00 a.m., he rolled up on the small farm and stables that his mom and Mac owned. He parked the truck and got out, looking out across the fenced-in paddocks, the near pastures, and beyond them, the famous rolling hills that defined the region. His mom, Jenny Turner, was a third-generation horse breeder. But after her divorce from Jock, and the devastating events that wrecked her health, she had abandoned the wealthy estate that she and Jock had created by merging their lucrative family interests. These days, she and Mac lived a simpler life, operating their small riding stables for the benefit of locals, and the throngs of tourists that toured the area each year. The pair also took in retired racehorses, put out to pasture after years of strenuous training and competition to enjoy their remaining, lazy days. Marcus eyed a trio of the equine retirees, grazing in a distant field, and then looked toward the stables. His mom and Mac, up since dawn, would still be in there, tending to the horses, in the never-ending routine of feeding, grooming, and readying the animals for visiting riders.

Marcus knew his folks would have heard his truck pull up and, right on cue, he saw them emerge from the stables. Both were dressed in faded jeans, flannel shirts, and sturdy work boots. Marcus winced when he saw his mom leaning heavily on her walking stick, as she made her way toward him. Her gait was worse than the last time he'd seen her, and despite her joy at welcoming him home, the strain in her face told him she was fighting chronic pain.

Striding toward Marcus, Mac reached out his arms to close the distance and embrace the young man he thought of as a son. "Great to have you home," he said. Despite a few signs that age was catching up with him, Mac, now almost sixty, still stood tall, lean, sinewy, and strong. He held the early morning visitor to the farm in a tight hug. Then he moved aside so Jenny, who had hustled, limping, to catch up, could wrap her arms around the son who towered over her, and press her cheek against his chest.

Marcus knew from the sharp way she inhaled that his mom was fighting back happy tears. "It's good to be home, Mom," he said and kissed the top of her head. As usual, her hair was pulled back in a ponytail that accentuated the high cheekbones of her strong, handsome face. Life outdoors and constant pain had etched more lines on it, and he noticed there were more gray streaks and silver threads in the thick auburn hair that had once been the envy of the county, but his mother, now in her mid-fifties, was still a beauty. Jenny Turner was quite tall, long-legged, and statuesque, even though these days she had to rely on a silver-capped cane to stand and walk. She held her son away from her with one arm to look at him and laughed. "You are too handsome for your own good."

"You gonna tell me why you summoned me, Mom?" Marcus asked.

"I will after breakfast. I've got it all set up, eggs, sausage, and biscuits." She took his arm and the three of them made their way indoors. Marcus inhaled the rich smell of leather, polish, and the horse tack that Mac had been cleaning in the mud room. He detected the faint odor of the two labs, Piper and Bridey, and the fried apples his mother baked in her famous pies. He was surrounded by the smells of country, of flowers and grass, of animals and home cooking, of furnishings and objects that had been handed down from one generation to another. All mixed together, these familiar scents invaded Marcus's nostrils and triggered memories of happy times and forgotten pleasures.

After breakfast, Marcus helped Jenny clean up while Mac headed back to the stables. When they were done, his mother gestured toward the door. "Let's take a walk."

"Isn't it more comfortable to sit?" he asked, keenly aware that each step his mother took was painful.

She shook her head. "I stiffen up when I sit too long. Moving about is the lesser of two evils."

The pair made their way outdoors, with Marcus careful to slow down to match his mother's limping gait. They walked in silence for a while, enjoying the beauty that captured them both every time they went out to meet it. Finally, his mother sat on a hay bale, next to a fence post, and Marcus pulled himself up to sit atop the fence, the way he used to when he was a boy. "Marcus, it's time to forgive," she said without preamble.

Marcus was silent, biting into the long stem of Kentucky rye grass he had plucked and placed between his teeth. He gazed at the distant hills as though the answer to all his problems might be found there. "I have forgiven, Mom," he said finally.

"Well then it's time to come home." When Marcus didn't answer but just went on chewing his grass and pondering the hills, Jenny continued. "Your father has been very ill. He can't manage the business like he used to, and it's too much for Dawson to handle alone. He needs you."

"I have a job up north, Mom. I can't just up and leave." Marcus heard how feeble and ridiculous he sounded, defending his two-bit career as an itinerant bar manager.

"You're thirty-five, Marcus. Running someone else's dive bar is not a career. Turner-Bell Estate is Jock's and my legacy and your inheritance. On the day you were born, barefoot and wearing nothing but a white cotton nightdress, I carried you out into the fields and stood among the horses. I wanted you to see with your newborn eyes why I brought you into this world. To give you the same happiness and purpose that I have known, and that my Pa, and his Pa before him, knew; the joy of raising horses, never far from the beauty of nature, or from the satisfaction of doing an honest day's work. I wanted you to have all the contentment that comes from falling into bed at night happy and exhausted, knowing the whole wonderful routine will begin again tomorrow."

"There are still things I have to take care of in New York," Marcus said. He was thinking of Polly, although he wanted to steer clear of this topic. His mother wouldn't take kindly to him falling for a married woman, even if she was headed for divorce.

"Marcus, you have been gone for ten years. Even the great Ulysses, who arguably had the most adventures of any man, real or fictional, returned home to Ithaca after ten long years of wandering." Marcus was forced to smile. His mother might be happiest when she was mucking out stables and caring for clapped-out horses, but she had a mighty intellect, a thirst for knowledge, and a strong love of the classics. When they were growing up, Jenny had made sure that her sons did horse work, schoolwork, and plenty of reading from the family's well-stocked library. No TV allowed. He looked at her now. He loved her too much to play games with her or dismiss her genuine concerns. "Mom, I've forgiven Dad. I really have. I know it falls to me to run the estate. I just don't think I can do it while he is still living there. Just because I've forgiven him doesn't mean I have to endure living and working around him."

Jenny winced at his words. "I understand, Marcus. I know how much what he did damaged you. It took me a long time to forgive him, but I have. All that ancient history is blood under the bridge. What hurts me now is having you so far away and watching Dawson struggle. He doesn't even have time to date! Your life is your own. If I thought you could find any real happiness outside of Kentucky, I would wish it for you with every breath, but I know that your heart is here. Since you were a kid, running Turner-Bell was your dream. I know you can't be happy living away from it."

"Being away is better than having to see that man every day." Marcus strained to keep his voice even. His mother had endured enough cruelty at the hands of his father. There was no need to bring their discussion to a boil and poke old wounds.

"Sometimes," Jenny said, "we become stuck in the past,

unable to let go of feelings and thoughts that have no place in our life anymore. Your reaction to how your father injured me was normal at the time, and for a good while after, but not letting go after all these years is not healthy, Marcus. You've put your life on hold. You're drifting, rootless, and it's no good." He couldn't deny that his mother spoke the truth. He saw her shift uncomfortably on the hay bale. Marcus jumped off the fence and reached out his hand to help her up. "Come on, let's head back."

As they walked slowly back to the house in subdued silence, Jenny linked his arm with hers. "I'm happy, Marcus. I love Mac and we have a good life here. Sure, all the trouble between your dad and me caused me a lot of suffering, but the price I paid to have the life I enjoy now was worth it. You don't have to punish your father on my account. You know, I would consider it a blessing if you could mend fences with him and put all of those ugly doings in the past where they belong."

He stroked her hand. "I'll think about what you said, Mom."

She let the subject drop, knowing it was best not to push him any further. "Good, I appreciate that. Your brother is coming for dinner. He's excited you're home."

After their walk, Marcus headed to the stable to help Mac finish up the chores. He knew the man he'd known his whole life as a surrogate father would keep his own counsel and not pry into the painful subjects that were hanging in the air. The two men worked in silence, giving a couple of mares a good brush. When they were done, Mac nodded toward the tack room. "Want to go for a ride?" After the long drive through the night, and the tense conversation with his mother, Marcus was exhausted, but he could think of nothing he would like better than a gallop through the open fields. He surveyed two rows of horses in their stalls before finally selecting Mister Sturdy, a handsome chestnut gelding, sixteen hands high. He saddled up, mounted and maintained a light trot until he was clear of the stable and its pastures. When he hit the unfenced fields at the outer limits of the farm, he broke into a gallop. Marcus had sat a horse before he could walk, and learned to gallop before he could run. He was at home on horseback. Almost like Centaur, the half man, half horse of Greek mythology, Marcus felt like he merged with any horse he mounted. No matter how large and fast the animal, or how dangerous the terrain, he was fearless, almost like the creature's legs were under his control, and riding was really no different than running on his own two limbs.

He rode and rode, with the summer wind blowing in his face, listening only to the sound of galloping hooves and the gelding's heavy breathing. Eventually, he slowed, inhaling the sweet odor that rose from the horse's warm flesh, as sweat glistened on the animal's glossy, chestnut coat. The rider felt relaxed, as though all the stress and claustrophobia he felt at being hemmed in, living in the shadows of a big city, had drained out of him and escaped through the action of his mount's galloping hooves. There was no getting away from it. This was where he belonged. Marcus coaxed the magnificent beast into a slow walk to cool him off, finally making his way up the long, straight drive bordered by white fencing. At the stable, he dismounted and watered the horse, untacking and curry combing the gelding before putting him away. "Good boy." He kissed the gentle creature's long nose and patted his flank as he left.

Inside, his mother had chicken sandwiches and fried apple pie waiting. As he entered the cozy farm kitchen, Marcus could hear her and Mac laughing together. Theirs was a true love story. It made him happy to think of his mother living out her final years with her soul mate—a man who was loyal and devoted to her happiness.

Marcus finished lunch, took a long shower and hit the sack for a nap so he'd be fresh for dinner with his brother. He fell into a deep sleep.

***

Marcus found himself sitting alone in a dark theater, watching a ballerina perform effortlessly on the stage with hypnotic grace. He recognized Polly and had to have her. He slowly left his seat and climbed onto the stage, but the dancer had disappeared into the shadows. Moving aside the thick velvet curtains, he tried to find her with no luck. When he finally gave up looking, he felt a hand reach out and caress his cheek. Polly stepped out from the shadows. Her hands stroked his body, like it was part of her dance. They recreated the passionate kiss they had shared outside the bar.

***

Marcus awoke, and a shudder of pleasure rippled through him.

Dinner was not until seven, but an excited Dawson showed up at six. After several hearty servings of Jenny's pot roast, Mac broke out the poker set for a game of Texas hold 'em. They played for jellybeans and Dawson cleaned up like a boss, winning every last sugary bean. "That's it, I'm out," Jenny announced. She leaned forward to rake back some of her youngest son's winnings then popped them into her mouth.

"Hey!" Dawson feigned outrage.

Jenny waved goodnight. "Son, I made up a bed in your old room in case you're too tired to drive back to Turner-Bell tonight." She leaned on her stick with one hand, and linked Mac's arm with her other, ready to tackle the stairs.

Dawson blew her a kiss. "Thanks, Mom, but I have to get back tonight so I can be up extra early tomorrow. We're shipping out a couple of fillies."

The evening had been fun. Jenny had been careful to keep the atmosphere light and avoid any heavy topics. Now, the two brothers sat, sipping bourbon at their mother's large kitchen table. It was the heart of the home. At this table, a family heirloom from her great-grandmother Celine, Jenny prepared food, set informal meals, did her reading, her paperwork, her mending, and her crafts. She always declared that if the whole house blew down and just this table was left standing, she could carry on as usual.

Marcus leaned back in his chair, knowing his kid brother was getting ready to petition him. And sure enough, now that they were alone, Dawson got straight after it. "Marcus, you know I don't wish you any disrespect, and I don't want to come off like I'm hounding you, but would you drive over to Turner-Bell tomorrow to have a meeting with Dad and me about the future of the farm? I sincerely understand if you don't want to do it, but would you just consider it, please?"

"I will drive over to Turner-Bell tomorrow," Marcus said.

Dawson couldn't believe his ears. For the last five years, he had been calling his brother every few months like clockwork, begging, cajoling, sweet talking, and nagging him to come home, or at least discuss the possibility. But as hard as Dawson had tried to persuade him, Marcus had resisted every ploy. Yet tonight, here he was, folding and accepting the invitation right out of the gate. "That's so great because Dad…" But before Dawson could finish, Marcus interrupted him.

"Dawson, didn't anyone ever teach you not to sell past the close?" Dawson smiled, drained his glass, and leaned in to give his brother a hug. "I'm headed out. I'll see you tomorrow at Turner-Bell. Shall we say after lunch?"

"After lunch is fine," Marcus agreed. He saw his brother out, switched off the lights, and made his way up the creaking staircase to bed. The windows were open, and he lay for a longtime listening to the katydids, letting the evening breeze caress his body, and thinking of Polly.

CHAPTER 8: CHRISSY

After her passionate kiss with Marcus outside the Oasis bar, Polly had headed home to the empty townhouse. She sat cross legged on her bed with a glass of wine and her laptop open, ready to investigate Chrissy Reynolds, but she was distracted. What she really wanted was to think about the exciting new man that fate had put on a collision course with her and her Subaru. He had done the impossible by arousing her even more than Christian ever had. How could that be? Maybe because what Marcus offered was more than just raw animal passion. With him, there was a promise of sex combined with respect, kindness, and tenderness. Every time she tried to put him out of her mind, her thoughts returned to their kiss, and the new possibilities that the future might hold, beyond her wrecked marriage. She knew she was vulnerable and needed to think clearly as she mapped out her next moves. Skipping from one relationship to another was a mistake and would distract from getting her life and her career back on track.

In the bar, Marcus had made a toast to reclaiming dreams. Polly's dream was dance and, eventually, love with a man she could trust. In that order. But before any of that could happen, she had to sort out the mess with Christian.

Until this was done, she couldn't begin to entertain getting involved with Marcus or anyone else.

Polly pushed aside distractions and focused on the task of tracking down Chrissy Reynolds. It wasn't hard. Marcus had said she was a local, and with just a few clicks, Polly was able to discover that Chrissy lived not far from the Oasis bar, and surprise, surprise, she worked in Christian's building. How like her husband to combine lust with convenience. *He's gone after some chick who works in the same office park so his affair doesn't mess up his routine.* She stopped to imagine him following Chrissy into one of the office building's white-tiled, sterile bathrooms for a quickie, and she let out a mirthless laugh. In a heartbeat, happiness could turn into pain, but then just as quickly, that pain could be transformed back into happiness. And it gave Polly great happiness to know she was moving on from Christian Caldwell's sordid sexual games and petty dictatorship.

Done with her sleuthing for the night, Polly relaxed and finally let thoughts of Marcus have free rein. She visualized his handsome face and strong body. For just a moment while they kissed, she had reached out and touched the hardness that strained in the crotch of his jeans, before quickly drawing back her hand. Now in the privacy of her bedroom, she slipped her hand beneath the elastic of her panties. In the parking lot, on full view to passersby and casual observers, she had been unable to give into her urges with Marcus. Lying on her bed, her hand between her thighs, she allowed her fantasy to play out, bringing herself close to climax again and again. Each time slowing down and taming her thoughts, only to let them loose again. Finally, after almost an hour, she let her fantasy of making love with Marcus peak with an intense shudder and a moan.

She carried her wine into the bathroom, lit lavender-scented candles, and took a long, satisfying soak, perfectly relaxed and ready for tomorrow. Over the last few days, she had felt ambushed, like life with its sordid revelations about Christian and his affairs had jumped her. But tomorrow, she would be the one to pounce.

As she dried herself and got ready for bed, Polly mapped out her next moves. She would continue to ignore Christian's calls and texts. They were coming thick and fast now, but she blithely disregarded them, breaking her habit of always answering within minutes of hearing from her husband. That would get him thinking. She could feel him trying to read what was happening on the home front as uncomfortable questions popped into his head. Why had Polly bailed on cooking a special dinner the night before he left on his trip? Why had she avoided sex and gone to sleep instead? Why was she ignoring him? Polly knew her husband was getting rattled, maybe even a little paranoid. She had heard almost nothing from him for the first two days he was gone, except for text reminders to fix the car. But this morning he had decided to call. When she didn't pick up, he had mounted a pressure campaign, bombarding her with messages that drove a constant pinging from her phone, until she'd finally turned off notifications. She hadn't bothered to listen to his voicemails either, but she imagined they were becoming more angry and dictatorial, the more she ignored him. She smiled. Yes, tomorrow she would keep icing Christian, but she would deal with the car. And she would pay Chrissy Reynolds a visit. With a satisfied sigh, Polly turned out the light and was soon sleeping like a baby.

***

The next morning, surrounded by the clattering sounds and chemical smells of the body shop, Polly watched Reggie bend over to examine the Subaru's smashed bumper. "I can't do it today because I have to order the parts," he explained, "but I can replace the broken headlight, so you won't have trouble with the cops, okay?" Polly agreed. The front end wasn't pretty, but as long as she was in no danger of getting a ticket, she was happy to wait until Reggie could schedule the repairs. In only minutes, he had replaced the light and was shaking her hand. "I'll call you when the parts arrive and you can bring it in."

"What do I owe you for the light?" she asked, as a mechanic began yelling for Reggie to come inspect the dents in the hood of a red Audi. "Pay me later," he called over his shoulder as he hurried off.

"Thanks!" Polly gave the horn two small taps as a goodbye and set off for her lunch appointment. Well, to be honest, it was more of an ambush than an appointment, but all is fair in love and war, or so she had heard.

**

Christian and Chrissy were a match made in heaven, Polly thought, as she waited in the car park, outside the office building where they both worked for different companies. Her husband was in marketing and his girlfriend was in sales, and together, the pair of them amounted to little more than a couple of smooth-talking con artists. Around a quarter past twelve, Chrissy emerged, dressed in her uniform of silk blouse, tight skirt, and high heels. She took off in her BMW with Polly once again on her tail. Soon it was clear that the blonde was headed for the Oasis bar. Once there, she parked, got out, and strolled into the bar. Polly waited a few minutes before going in after her. She knew Marcus was out of town, so there was no chance she'd run into him. Inside, she found Chrissy sitting at the bar with a glass of white wine. Polly eased herself onto a stool right next to her, and Chrissy gave her side eye, annoyed that some woman was sitting so close, when there were plenty of vacant seats in the half-empty watering hole.

Polly had dressed up in a belted summer dress with shoestring straps that showed off her toned body and curves. Her hair was loose and curled, and she had taken extra care in applying her makeup. Chrissy was sneaking sideways glances to check her out, and Polly wondered if she recognized her as the woman that Marcus had kissed in the parking lot yesterday. Sheri made her way over to take her order. "Wow, you look lovely today! What can I get you?" When she returned with Polly's glass of red, she set it down and appraised the two good-looking women perched side by side. The boss certainly was a chick magnet. He had women lined up at the bar, like birds on a wire, just hanging around, hoping to see him. "If either of you are looking for Marcus, he's out of town," she announced before walking away.

Polly took a few leisurely sips of her red wine. In no rush to engage her husband's mistress, she waited instead for curiosity to get the better of the woman. Chrissy shifted on the bar stool, occasionally looking at Polly's wedding rings before she finally spoke. "I haven't seen you in here before. How do you know Marcus?"

"Oh, my car hit his in the parking lot, and he's been helping me schedule the repairs."

"Bummer." Her curiosity satisfied, Chrissy turned away again.

"My husband likes everything to be perfect," Polly said nonchalantly. "The busted fender is driving him crazy."

"Then why doesn't *he* take care of it?" Chrissy said emphatically, tossing her head in a gesture of girl power and solidarity.

Polly was unhurried when she replied. "Believe me, he would take care of it, but he's out of town for four days on a tour of his agency's Midwest clients." She knew she'd said just enough to set Chrissy Reynold's mind racing, and sure enough, the blonde immediately drained her glass, stood up, and retrieved her Chanel bag from the hook under the bar where she'd hung it.

"Aw, don't go," Polly said with a smile. "I thought we could swap stories about having sex with Chris in public bathrooms."

***

Chrissy Reynolds worked in pharmaceutical sales, and was one of her company's top performers. She took regular courses on how to be a killer in business and life. How to believe in herself, never take no for an answer, and ABC— Always Be Closing. Her mornings began with the daily affirmations she recited to reassure herself that she was on top, that no deal was too big, no goal too daring, no competition too steep, and no situation too thorny that she couldn't solve it. One of Chrissy Reynolds' favorite affirmations was "never let them see you sweat." With this in mind, she now looked Christian Caldwell's wife in her undeniably lovely, green eyes. Of course, she was aware Chris had a wife, but she had zero interest in knowing anything about her. Why should she? Chris was handsome and a fun way to spend time when she wasn't off closing lucrative deals. Sex with him was off-the-charts great, including in restrooms, where the thrill quotient was high, but the comfort level was low. Truth be told, though, Chrissy was tiring of Christian and was now much more interested in Marcus Bell.

The hunky bar manager liked to play the part of free spirit and rolling stone. He might be slumming it in the Oasis, but Chrissy knew he was actually Kentucky royalty, and backed by a family dynasty worth millions that was legend in horse-breeding circles. She'd found this out a few weeks back during a night of heavy drinking at the bar, when Marcus had loosened up a bit and let slip a few nuggets about his upbringing. Since then, Chrissy had decided that his background and pedigree made Marcus Bell perfect marriage material for her. Yes, she could definitely see herself ensconced in the bosom of his well-heeled family, at the top of Kentucky society, and the exclusive world of horse racing. She could easily play the part of lady of the manor, who lived in couture fashion and paraded around in one-of-a-kind hats at the Kentucky Derby, drinking Pimm's Cup in the Winners' Enclosure.

Chrissy wasn't worried or embarrassed that she'd been

caught having an affair by her lover's wife. She could easily cut loose from any tacky drama. What bothered her was that, apparently, Mrs. Caldwell knew Marcus, and Chrissy did not relish her future husband knowing the details of her fling with some hotshot from the office park. Sure, she'd flirted with other men in front of Marcus. She'd even brought Christian to the Oasis a few times. It didn't hurt for Marcus to see how other men drooled over her. Still, she'd rather he not know about her habit of grabbing sex with married men in bathrooms, cars, and pricey hotel rooms.

As Chrissy stood, coolly assessing Polly, it occurred to her that the striking brunette looked familiar. The day before, she had watched Marcus kissing a woman in the parking lot. Kissing her so passionately that he still had a raging hard-on when he came back into the bar. It was common knowledge the eligible bachelor had enjoyed a few casual hook-ups over the last year, but judging by their steamy lip-lock, this latest one looked to be a real turn-on. Chrissy was studying Polly more closely now. The mystery woman yesterday wore a ponytail and workout gear. Her look was casual and all natural, no make-up. The woman next to her, Chris's wife, was dressed up, beautiful, and low-key glamorous, but the resemblance between Miss Sporty from yesterday and the glamazon perched on the barstool today was unmistakable. Finally, as the truth hit her, Chrissy slapped the bar. "Helping you with car repairs, my ass! You were the one making out with Marcus yesterday after you left the bar with him."

Polly smiled. She knew Chrissy had gotten an eyeful of her clinch with Marcus and might recognize her, but what difference did it make? She'd made up her mind to leave Chris and what was he going to say if Chrissy spilled the beans to him? "My mistress says she caught you kissing some guy she wants to screw." Polly laughed and Chrissy scowled. "What's so funny?"

"Oh, nothing." Polly patted the stool her neighbor had vacated. "Listen, don't run off. Let me buy you a drink and we can discuss things like grown women." She raised an eyebrow to underscore the invitation. To her surprise, Chrissy sat down again. She was as eager to know about this creature that had captivated Marcus Bell as Polly was to know about her.

As Chrissy relaxed and opened up, Polly began to grasp the extent of her husband's cheating. "Do you know that Chris had sex with your wedding planner and your bookkeeper?" Chrissy asked.

"I didn't know that, but they couldn't have enjoyed it that much," Polly said.

"Why do you say that?"

"Because neither of them gave me a discount," Polly deadpanned, and Chrissy laughed, slapping the bar again. Sheri watched them from the other end and wondered what they were up to.

Polly saw what made Chrissy different from Christian's other conquests. His newest mistress had beaten him at his own game. The pair had met because they worked in the same building. When their flirtation quickly turned physical, they both agreed that they were only in it for the sex. Chrissy, Polly could tell, was even more ambitious and self-directed than Christian. She wanted sex on demand with no strings, not the drudgery of a tedious, long-term relationship. It must have pricked Christian's ego that he couldn't wrap his latest woman around his finger and have her begging for more. Chrissy was a successful and headstrong boss-lady. She, not the guys she picked up, made the rules in her life. Polly understood what made Chris tick. When he couldn't control Chrissy, it followed that he'd scheme and maneuver until she was eating out of his hand. He wouldn't dump her until he'd fully owned her.

"No offense," Chrissy leaned in conspiratorially, "but I make twice as much money as Christian. I live in a gated community. I can afford luxury fashion and cars. Outside of the sheets, your husband has little to offer me."

"Me neither," Polly quipped, and Chrissy cracked up

again.

Looking back, Polly recognized how Christian had become preoccupied with love bombing and captivating Chrissy because elusive, casual sex with her was no longer enough for him. That's why he'd gotten careless and begun staying out late, rousing his wife's unwanted suspicions. "Chris was always guarding his phone," she confided to Chrissy. "Probably nervous I might find his text messages to you."

"You wanna see 'em?" Chrissy took out her phone.

"Sure." Polly felt queasy, but she leaned in to eye the random texts that Chris's mistress pulled up. "Can't live without you…I want more…Been thinking about you all day…Wife is working all afternoon, want to check into a hotel?"

"Not very imaginative." Polly tried to sound cool, fighting the reflex to shut down, as she read the messages. The details of her husband's betrayal dripped like a corrosive acid on her life, destroying her illusion of a marriage she had thought of as safe and loving.

"That's what I thought," Chrissy agreed. "I told him it was getting boring."

"And what did he say?"

"He said he was going to leave you and make a great life for us." Chrissy's tone was matter-of-fact. She was starting to think Polly was pretty cool. She was spilling facts about the affair, not to wound the gullible wife, but only because they were the truth. "I hope that doesn't hurt," she added solicitously.

"No, it doesn't," Polly lied. "And I hope it doesn't hurt when I tell you that the only reason Christian wants you is because he can't have you, and as soon as he can have you, he won't want you anymore. Chris has a carefully mapped out, five-year game plan. I am in his plan because I am a game piece he can move around. You are not in his long-term plan, because you'll never be a game piece he can move around."

"True story." Chrissy raised her hand to high-five Polly. "You don't have to be a game piece either, Polly."

"True story," Polly said, and the two women slapped their palms together.

Christian's obsession with his latest piece-of-ass had made him sloppy and undisciplined and set off alarm bells that had woken Polly up from her trance. An hour later, when she stood to leave the bar, she shook Chrissy's hand. "I want to thank you, Chrissy Reynolds."

"For what, Polly Caldwell?"

"Because you've been the perfect alarm clock."

"And what time is it?" Chrissy asked.

"Time to clean house and recapture dreams," Polly declared, and then walked out of the bar, leaving Christian's mistress on her barstool. "She's a cool chick," Chrissy said grudgingly to Sheri, who had come to collect their glasses. She nodded in agreement. Chrissy ordered more wine. As she drank alone, she fervently hoped that should the dancer with the stunning looks and killer body decide to kick Christian to the curb, she wouldn't turn out to be stiff competition in the Marcus Bell stakes.

CHAPTER 9: CHRISTIAN

Jay, the director of StepWorks Dance Company, walked into the Beat It studio with flyers advertising auditions for the company's upcoming revival of *Chicago*. Seeing him enter, Polly felt awkward. She knew the talented director forgave her for ditching his tour, but she'd never been able to shake the feeling that she'd let him down. She'd certainly let herself down.

"Hey, mind if I put these up?" Jay waved the flyers.

"Go for it."

He worked quietly, pinning his notices on the studio's bulletin boards, and once he was done, he made a beeline for the good-looking proprietor, who was finishing up her monthly billing. "How's business, Polly?" he asked.

She looked up from her laptop. "It's good."

"I hear you're as good at teaching as you were at performing," Jay said, and she smiled, a little embarrassed. "You know, you were probably the best Velma Kelly I ever saw live on stage," he continued. "Certainly the best I ever worked with."

"Right up until the point where I left your tour in Paris without a Velma Kelly."

Jay shrugged. "That's why we have understudies. You're

being too hard on yourself. I think you did what was best for everyone, and it was a great break for Lucy Neville. Graduating from understudy to take over a lead role for most of the European performances really launched her career. She's out in LA and very hot right now."

So her bad luck had been Lucy's lucky break, Polly thought. She realized that Jay had always assumed it was her injury that kept her from rejoining the company. He didn't know she'd abandoned the tour because of Christian. *Leaving because you're injured is different than skipping out because your fiancé demands it,* she thought. *One is honorable, the other is weak.* "I loved working with you and the company," Polly said. "It was a highlight for me, and I still feel like I owe you for giving me my big break."

"Well, if you owe me, why don't you come help me with this production?" Jay asked casually. He'd come to the studio with an agenda, intent on accomplishing more than just pinning up flyers. "My choreographer is out on maternity leave until fall, and I need a replacement to get me through auditions and the rehearsal phase. I'm sure we can make the schedules work. How about it?"

"Do it, Polly," a voice called from the doorway. Maria had walked in on the conversation. "I can pick up the slack here, or get someone to help cover your classes."

"I'll pay you," Jay said. "You know the going rate for choreographers isn't high round here, probably not as much as you make teaching, but I can promise you a lot of fun."

Polly did not doubt the fun part. She looked from Maria, who was nodding her head vigorously, to Jay, who was waiting for her answer. "I appreciate the offer. Is it okay if I take a day or so to think about it?"

"Sure," Jay said as he made his way out. "Today's Friday, and auditions start next Wednesday, so I need your answer no later than Monday."

"Okay," Polly agreed, as she checked the details on the flyer she was holding: Casting performers for the musical *Chicago*. Lead and ensemble roles for a musical based on the

Broadway show and film of the same name. Seeking local applicants for the New York area. She folded the notice and put it in her bag, just as her phone rang. It was a local number she didn't recognize, but she answered it anyway. "Hello?"

"Is this Polly?" The voice was vaguely familiar.

"It is. Who's this?"

"It's Chrissy Reynolds."

"Oh." Standing in the studio, dressed down in her sweats, Polly was painfully aware of how the emotional high that had come from confronting Chrissy yesterday had somehow evaporated overnight. She had awoken up early, wondering how on earth she'd worked up the nerve to confront and chat up her husband's mistress. Then, she'd spent the rest of the morning dreading the fall-out that was sure to follow their conversation.

"I'm just calling to tell you I broke up with your husband about an hour ago," Chrissy said, as though it was perfectly normal to give your lover's wife a blow-by-blow account of developments in the adulterous relationship going on behind her back.

"You did?" Polly could feel knots starting to tie themselves in her stomach.

"I did. Christian rang me as he was headed for the airport to fly home. He called to tell me, and I quote, 'I've missed you like crazy. Can't wait to get my hands on you. How about we sneak off someplace tomorrow at lunchtime?'"

Hearing the latest details of how Christian offered sex to his mistress felt like another slap in Polly's face. Having made up her mind to leave him, she wanted to pretend that she'd come to terms with his betrayal, but she hadn't. She thought if she could make light of his "indiscretions" and somehow laugh them off over drinks with his mistress, it would shield her from the hurt, but it didn't. Her husband's infidelity was crushing.

"You there?" Chrissy asked when Polly didn't answer.

"Yes, I'm here. What did you tell him?" Polly asked,

almost certain she didn't want to know.

"I told him that I hung out with his hot wife yesterday and decided that I like her more than I like him." Chrissy sounded like she was jettisoning a bad business deal she'd lost interest in. Polly remembered how the sales rep had summed up her arrangement with Christian yesterday. "Let's face it, outside of the sheets, there's not much Chris can do for me."

"And what did Christian have to say about that?" Polly was doing her best not to react but simply to extract the information she knew would further turn her world upside down.

"I don't know," Chrissy said. "I hung up before he could say anything. I gave Chris the relevant information. How he reacts to it is none of my concern. Listen, I have to run to a meeting. I just wanted to give you the heads up."

"Thanks," Polly said, but Chrissy had already hung up. *Thanks? Did I just thank the woman who's been sleeping with my husband for breaking up with him?* She dropped onto a chair. Maria looked worried. "Polly, are you okay, you've gone pale?"

***

On the ride home later that day, Polly couldn't shake an intense feeling of foreboding. It was nearly 5:00 p.m. when she turned the key in the front door lock, fully expecting to find an irate Christian inside, but there was no sign of him, except for a bouquet of white roses that stood in her cut-glass vase on the kitchen island. Propped against the vase was a card.

"I've missed you like crazy. Can't wait to get my hands on you. See you when I get back from the gym. Be ready."

Christian's written love note to his wife was almost identical to what he had told his mistress when he'd called her that morning. Polly stared at the card in disbelief. *He knows Chrissy and I spoke, because she told him, and still he has the balls to leave flowers and a cocky message.* She tossed the card in the garbage and examined the expensive bouquet. *Flowers? He honestly believes he can charm his way out of this. He thinks I'm stupid enough to swallow whatever story he concocts to cover his ass. And why wouldn't he? Swallowing his crap is what I usually do.*

Polly felt paralyzed, unsure what to do next. Christian would be back within the hour to start wrapping her in a sticky web of lies, excuses, and manipulation, and she feared that like always, she'd be no match for him. But then it dawned on her that for Christian to control her, she had to be in the same room with him. For the last four days, while he had been out of town, she had ignored him completely. Her silence had infuriated him, but what could he do about it? As long as she kept out of her husband's way, she would have the upper hand. *If I stay here,* she thought, *I'll be like the mongoose that gets hypnotized and eaten by the snake. He'll lie, cajole, and try to explain away his affair with Chrissy. He'll claim it was meaningless, or a misunderstanding, or even just a figment of my imagination. It will be all "he said, she said." He'll bend over backward to make me believe none of it happened, or if it did happen that it meant nothing, while he begs for forgiveness and another chance that I don't want to give him.*

She knew Christian couldn't stop her from leaving the marriage, but he could slow her down, cause her to stumble, and make it hard for her to move forward and break free of him. She was suddenly gripped by decisiveness. She had to get out before he returned. But where would she go? She'd figure that out later. She sprinted upstairs to the bedroom, grabbed a bag from the closet, packed enough clothes and toiletries for a few days, and hurried out.

Polly drove around for a bit to calm her nerves. Going to her parent's place was the obvious next move, but she decided against it. Before she could tell them she was leaving Christian, she first had to make sense of it all and figure out how to explain the sorry state of affairs to her friends and family. And besides, when Chris realized she'd left, the first place he'd go looking for her was at her parent's. She knew that before her lying husband could get to them, she should call them first without giving too much away and alarming them. She forced herself to smile so she'd sound cheery and rang her mother.

"Hi sweetheart, I was just thinking about you." As always, Annie's greeting was warm and loving. It made Polly want to turn back the clock to a time when she lived in the midst of her happy family. Back then, there had been no lies, deception, or baffling events to trip her up. Life had been simple and straightforward. She had trusted the people around her, and relied on herself to make good decisions. "Hey Mom, I've had a bit of an argument with Christian," she said casually. "I had a fender bender the other day in a parking lot, nothing serious, but I tore up the bumper on my car. Chris is being really pissy about it, and I'm in no mood to deal with him. I'm going to check into a hotel on his credit card and treat myself to some me time until he stops being in such a snit. You know what he's like."

"Why don't you come over here for the night?" Annie asked.

"Nah, Chris just got back from a business trip, and I wouldn't put it past him to come by and sweet talk me into coming home. I want to let him stew for a bit."

"Are you sure everything is okay?"

Polly let her guard down and sounded weary. "I'm fine, Mom. I'm just sick of Chris bossing me around and always getting his way. I want to teach him a lesson."

"Well," Annie said, "you know I don't like Christian stressing you with his nonsense, but I'm glad to hear you finally pushing back on the overbearing jerk!"

"Please, Mom, I don't want to get into it," Polly moaned.

"Okay then," Annie said. "You go chill out at a nice hotel, but please text me to let me know where you are. Christian won't get it out of me if he calls."

Fifteen minutes later, Polly checked into a nearby Hilton. She dropped her bag and sprawled on one of the room's two double beds. The hotel overlooked Route 1, and Polly

knew a little ways down that main drag was the Oasis bar.
Marcus should be back from his trip to Kentucky by now,
and she was free from Christian's clutches, at least for
tonight. She was in a dilemma. She wanted to see Marcus,
forget the mess she was in, and lose herself for a few hours
in his company. Yes, she'd just met him, but she knew from
their conversation in the bar that he was honest and decent,
that she could trust him. Could lean on the friendship he
offered her, as she extricated herself from the sewer her
marriage had become. But another voice told her to stay put.
It was long past time for her to stand on her own two feet
again. Hadn't relying too heavily on a man created the mess
she found herself in now? Her phone pinged. A text from
Christian. Don't read it. Of course, he'd be back from the
gym and annoyed that she wasn't home. Maybe he'd noticed
she'd packed a bag and left. She stood up, certain she
couldn't sit alone in a hotel room all night while her
wheedling husband bombarded her with messages that
wore down her resolve. She freshened up in the bathroom
and set out.

***

Friday nights at the Oasis were always busy, and this
Friday night was no exception. Polly walked in to find the
place packed, standing room only. Sheri was working
alongside a bartender Polly hadn't seen before, and there
was no sign of Marcus. It was ten minutes before she could
even get Sheri's attention to order a beer, and the harried
bartender was too rushed to give her more than a quick nod
hello. Now what? If Marcus was around, he was someplace
out of sight. Polly was uncomfortable, crammed like a
sardine into the hot, sweaty bar, fending off hungry looks
from guys on the prowl. As they talked work or sports with
friends, she could see the bro brigade scanning the room,
deploying their radar to spot which women were open for
business. Another fifteen minutes went by, and Sheri,

scrambling to serve customers who were standing two deep at the bar, finally came within earshot. Polly managed to yell over the rock song blasting from the speaker above her head. "Sheri, where's Marcus?"

"What?" Sheri cupped her ear with one hand as she grabbed for a vodka bottle with the other.

"Where's Marcus?" Polly shouted louder, mouthing the words as clearly as she could. Sheri thrust her thumb upward and Polly squinted to convey her confusion. "What?"

"Upstairs in his apartment," Sheri yelled, making the same upward motion with her thumb. Then, the bartender shot Polly a look that made it clear she was overwhelmed serving thirsty hoards, and in no mood to deal with wenches who were on the hunt for a piece of her boss.

Polly left the hot, noisy, overcrowded bar and stood on the sidewalk where a light breeze cooled her. It hadn't occurred to her that Marcus might live above the Oasis. Why would it? She barely knew him. But here she was, on the run from her husband, staring up at a light in a second-story window, in hopes of finding the man who was becoming something of an infatuation.

Polly walked up and down. She scanned the store fronts for a way to reach the upper floor of the bar that was sandwiched between a deli and a dry cleaners, but she couldn't find one. Could the upstairs apartment only be accessed from inside the bar? She took a deep breath, went back inside, and pushed her way through the packed room until she made it to the restrooms at the far end. She saw stairs descending, presumably to a basement, but no stairs leading up to a second floor. She did notice, however, that the back door had been propped open with a beer crate to ventilate the hot room. Exiting through the door, she found herself on the backside of the building. She peered through the window of an adjacent door. Stairs led to a small landing and what looked like doors to two apartments. Bingo! She guessed Marcus lived in 2A, the one to the left and directly above the bar.

The front door of 2A had been left slightly ajar. Polly knocked lightly and called out softly, "Hello." No answer. Inside, she found a decent-sized living room, nicely furnished with high-end furniture, framed photos, and various trophies from the horse racing world. A galley kitchen was separated by a wall, with a pass-through opening to the room's small dining area. Down a narrow hallway, she noticed a half-open door. Guessing it was Marcus's bedroom, she walked gingerly toward it, like a trespasser afraid of getting caught. She was struck by the absurdity of her situation, prowling uninvited around the apartment of a man she hadn't known existed five days ago. Still, she was here now. She'd rather deal with the embarrassment of showing up unannounced than heading back to the empty hotel room, where she'd fret about Christian and the havoc that her chat with Chrissy had no doubt caused. Polly reached the bedroom and stood still, quietly listening for a moment. When she finally put her head around the door, she was confronted with yet another horrendous surprise.

***

The ride back from Kentucky had been smooth until Marcus was within fifty miles of home, and then he'd crawled along in bumper-to-bumper traffic for two long hours. When he finally parked in the back of his building, he could tell from the noise and raucous voices coming through its open back door that the bar was jumping. He'd hoped to be back sooner to help with the rush. He sighed. It couldn't be helped. He grabbed his bag, pushed his way inside, and caught Sherri's eye. Behind the bar, she and Jeremy were fighting a losing battle to keep up with the crowd of thirsty revelers, who were cutting loose and drinking hard after a long work week. He held up ten fingers to signal that he'd be back in ten minutes, or the time it took to grab a quick shower, wash off the road, and change into fresh clothes.

He bounded up the stairs to his apartment and found his front door slightly open. Nothing unusual. He kept a supply of premium liquors in his apartment closet, and Jeremy had probably been up to fetch a few bottles to restock the bar. Marcus made a beeline for the bathroom to turn on the shower and then crossed the hall to his bedroom. In a rush, he yanked off his T-shirt, revealing a flat, six-pack stomach, and muscular arms and chest. In the dim light of the bedroom, he didn't notice the figure sprawled on his bed until she spoke. "I brought you a welcome home present." Chrissy Reynolds wore only a black corset that pushed up her breasts, failed to cover her crotch, and was cut high to show off her long, spectacular legs. She was lying on her side, propped on an elbow, while her other hand dangled a bottle of Kentucky bourbon, just one of the gifts she intended to offer Marcus Bell that night.

CHAPTER 10: FLIGHT

The hostess ushered Polly and Danelle into a cozy booth in the bistro that was located in the heart of Danelle's quaint Connecticut town. It was Monday evening, and Danelle had suggested the two friends go out for a nice dinner like old times, while Lou Senior watched the baby. They ordered wine and looked over a menu inspired by French country cuisine. Not feeling hungry, Polly quickly settled on croque monsieur with a side of field greens, but when the waitress came to take their order, she found Danelle poring over the menu, performing an almost forensic analysis of its offerings. "Need more time?" the waitress said, pen and pad at the ready, but perfectly prepared to come back later. "Yes, please," Danelle said and smiled at Polly, who looked nervous and impatient, like she was ready to race through dinner and rush back to the house to pace up and down, too antsy to sit still for more than a minute. She was anxious and who could blame her?

"What?" Danelle asked with mock indignation as Polly gave her stink eye for taking too long to order. "Since Louis Junior was born, I barely get out. Let a girl relish a good dinner, why don't you?"

After fleeing Marcus's place on Friday night, Polly had

rushed, burning with humiliation, back to the hotel, where she'd finally managed to fall asleep at around 3:00 a.m. When she surfaced from a fitful sleep just a few hours later, a name popped into her head—Danelle. Of course, she could come and stay for the weekend, her friend had said when Polly called her from the road. In the drama of the present, the past had been forgotten, and their friendship had kicked back in stronger than ever.

Polly had shown up on Danelle's doorstep on Saturday morning, looking and acting like a basket case. Over the course of the weekend, she briefed her old friend on the mess her marriage was in but skipped all mention of Marcus Bell. She had no firm plans, she explained, but she was certain that she wanted to leave Christian. She was equally certain he wouldn't let her go without a fight.

"Christian likes his coin too much," Danelle said when they discussed the emotional and financial cost a divorce would bring. "He's not gonna let some divorce lawyers bleed your bank account dry."

"His bank account," Polly corrected her. "Everything's in his name, the cars, the townhouse. I'm the lowly dance instructor, remember? And he's the guy earning the big money, who was gonna make a great life for *us*. From what I've read, the courts might force him to share proceeds from any sale of the townhouse, but he'll probably get to keep all the money he made while we were married."

The waitress served their food. Danelle had finally selected boeuf bourguignon, before changing her order to steak frites, and then changing it back to boeuf bourguignon. "So, Chrissy the side piece didn't share Christian's reaction after she told him the two of you had drinks and girl talk?" she asked.

"She told him we'd met, but hung up on him before he could say anything." Next, Polly imitated Chrissy's super bitchy announcement: "I gave Chris the relevant information. How he reacts to it is none of my concern."

Danelle cut into her beef. "She sounds like a complete

96

narcissist."

Polly gave an exaggerated nod. "Chris has finally met his match with that one. She was all high and mighty, letting me know that she made more money than him, could afford more toys than him, and that outside of the sheets, she didn't need him for anything and was bored with him." As she talked, Polly pantomimed Chrissy's speech from the bar, gesturing with her fork, like she was Marie Antoinette directing the peasants to eat cake. Danelle smirked, and Polly set down her fork, looking serious again. "Danelle, there is something I didn't tell you."

"What?" Danelle's eyes narrowed, and she stopped eating, her own fork caught halfway between the plate and her mouth. Polly fessed up to meeting Marcus and her feelings for him. She described the small collision in the parking lot, how he'd refused to make a claim on her insurance, and offered to help her find a repair shop. She explained the instant connection she felt with the gorgeous horse breeder turned bar manager, as they sipped beer and bourbon over a meandering conversation. She tried to convey how their goodbye kiss had aroused her, and kicked off obsessive thoughts about what life would be like if they could be together. A fantasy she knew, but such a satisfying one.

Danelle leaned back and sipped her wine. "I know I'm supposed to give you all kinds of lectures about the dangers of rebound relationships, and not jumping out of the frying pan into the fire, but sometimes things happen that push us into taking a leap that's long overdue."

Polly nodded in agreement. "There's more," she said.

"More?" Danelle lifted one of her exquisitely shaped eyebrows.

"Chrissy Reynolds has the hots for Marcus. She saw us talking in the bar, followed us outside, and watched us kiss in the parking lot." Polly exhaled, relieved to be sharing the most troublesome chapter of the saga.

"He's not into her is he?" Danelle asked.

"Well, that's the tricky part?"

"It gets trickier?" Danelle said sarcastically.

"On Friday night, after I checked into the Hilton, I went looking for Marcus in his apartment above the bar."

"He lives above the bar?" Danelle said, as though struck by how much it must suck to live and work in the same place, where you could never get away from the grind.

"Yes, he lives above the bar, and when I went up there, the door was open so I knocked and went in. And in the bedroom, laid on the bed, naked except for a corset, was Chrissy Reynolds."

"So horse guy *is* into her?" Danelle said, and Polly watched her friend's eyes narrow again, like she suspected Marcus might not be the knight in shining armor Polly made him out to be.

"He told me he wasn't into her when I asked him about her in the parking lot, before we kissed," Polly said.

"And what did he say when you found them together?"

"He wasn't in the bedroom when I found her all splayed out in heat."

"Not there? Where was he?"

"I don't know. In the bathroom probably, getting ready to rock Chrissy Reynold's world with mind-blowing sex. I ran out as soon as I saw Miss Hotter than July posing on the bed. I didn't hang around long enough for him to walk in and catch me making a fool of myself."

"Did Chrissy say anything?" Danelle probed.

"No, she just gave me a look."

"What kind of look?"

"The kind of look that says 'I have both of your men right where I want them'."

"What a low-down slut!" Danelle announced.

"Well, I can't blame Marcus for sleeping with the low-down slut, because I made it clear to him that I am unavailable. I'm otherwise engaged, trying to escape the fifth circle of hell that is my marriage to a serial cheater."

Polly glanced at her phone which had become a torture

device now that it was constantly blowing up with calls and texts from Christian she left unanswered. She saw the latest text was from her mom.

Mom- Polly, please call us immediately. Christian just left, very upset, because apparently, you're having an affair.

CHAPTER 11: FACING THE MUSIC

After their drink together at the Oasis, Chrissy had decided she quite liked Polly and felt sorry for her, sort of. The pretty dancer couldn't be too smart though because she'd married a dog. Any woman with an ounce of smarts could tell right away exactly who and what Chris was. Christian Caldwell was not marriage material. He was the hot-sex guy you keep around to spice things up with quickies in public places—restrooms, dimly lit bars, in the backseat of cabs, or the supply closet at the office. Marcus Bell, on the other hand, was marriage material. Good looking, check. Wealthy family, check. High social status, check. He might be fronting, for now, as a boho bar guy, but it was clear he was getting tired of his latest gig and planning to head back to Kentucky, where Chrissy planned to join him, preferably sooner rather than later. Of course, once they were officially together, she'd have to commute for a bit until she ditched her job. She was a top performer, great at selling and closing deals, but she was sick of the airports and the grind. She loved the money, but she was bored with the work and ready to give it up. Her main focus now was selling Marcus Bell on the idea that they should be together.

Initially, Chrissy had decided she wouldn't tell Christian that she had seen his wife playing tongue hockey with the Oasis bar manager, in a public parking lot of all places. When he called her from the airport, her goal had been simply to end their relationship, and get off the phone before her ditched lover had a chance to object. Using the excuse that his wife had found out about their affair was the perfect way for her to be rid of him and free to concentrate on Marcus. She wanted Christian in the dark about her plans for Marcus so he wouldn't screw them up. That meant it was better to stay silent about the whole Marcus-Polly incident. Aside from sucking face in the parking lot, Chrissy was pretty sure there wasn't much between the pair. Marcus had admitted as much when she questioned him about Polly and *that* kiss. He'd waved it off as no big deal, telling the same story Polly had. They'd had a minor collision, he felt bad and was helping to get her car fixed. "A Subaru is no match for a pick-up," he'd joked nervously.

"Well, if a kiss like that is how you help a girl with repairs, may I direct you to my new BMW? The engine light keeps coming on." Chrissy's look told Marcus that if he gave her the nod, she'd strip down and be all over him like a bad rash. "It's probably a glitch in the car's software," he said, ducking her come-on. "You should call BMW service."

So, Chrissy had decided not to snitch about the kiss to Christian, but then Friday night happened, and Miss Polly had walked into Marcus's bedroom, looking like she had the same thing on her mind as Chrissy—seduction. The encounter lasted only seconds, as the two women said nothing and just stared at each other. Sprawled on the bed, Chrissy had fixed Polly with a look that said, "Your yoga pants and a ponytail are no match for this body in this corset." And then she'd watched her mortified rival turn on her heels and scamper out, leaving Chrissy to wait and greet Marcus with her irresistible surprise.

When Chrissy left Marcus's place later that night, feeling a little bruised and worse for wear, she'd come up with a plan to shut Polly down. She'd convince Christian that his wife was in a hot and heavy affair with Marcus. She was looking forward to watching him squirm when he learned that two could play the adultery game. Then, she'd leave her ex-lover to deal with his annoying wife. Polly had asked for it. She should have stayed in her lane and backed off pursuing the eligible bar manager. Instead, she had left Chrissy with no choice but to protect the prize she'd set her sights on—Marcus. "No deal is too big to close. No objection is too hard to overcome. I get what I want, and I never let them see me sweat." Chrissy repeated her mantra, as she scrambled to locate Christian's number that she'd already deleted from her phone.

***

By late Tuesday morning, Polly was back from Danelle's place and sitting in her mother's kitchen, trying to explain just how and why her life had turned into such a tragic clown car. Her dad was at work. Patrick liked to leave the emotional dramas to his wife. Annie could bottom line it for him when he came home, and by then, she would have hatched a plan to set things to rights.

"I'm not the one having an affair, Mom," Polly insisted. "Christian is. He's a serial cheater."

"Then who's the guy you were caught kissing in the parking lot?" Annie was somehow more concerned about her daughter smooching a stranger in broad daylight, than the fact that her son-in-law was a chronic womanizer.

"He's the guy whose truck I hit with my car," Polly said.

Annie made a face. "Oh, so you paid for the damage with sexual favors? What happened to car insurance?"

"Ha-ha," Polly scoffed. Her mother had always been quick with the one-liners. "I was in a vulnerable state when I found out Christian is cheating, and the truck guy is really cute. We met for a drink in the bar where he works and wound up sharing a one-off kiss on the spur of the moment.

That's all there is to it. Happened once. Won't happen again." She didn't share how that kiss was all she could think about, and how crushed she was that Marcus had turned his attention elsewhere—to Chrissy. It looked like when he'd seen her in a corset, she'd turned out to be his type after all. *I wonder if he's into lingerie like Christian is,* she thought, before noticing her mom was nodding sympathetically, like she understood Polly's reasons for kissing some random guy, even if she didn't approve.

An hour later, Polly had told Annie her plans for the near future. Divorce definitely, and probably a short stay with her parents while she got her act together, plus a serious rethink of her career.

"Well, I hate to say I told you so," Annie said when she'd finished interrogating her daughter.

"You never said I told you so," Polly declared.

"Well, I may not have said it, but I *thought* it plenty of times," Annie said, and they both laughed. "It's your life, but I never thought Christian was right for you. I resent how he undermined your career, decided how you live your life, dictated when you can have children, where you live, what you spend your money on."

Polly groaned. "Please Mom, you make me sound like a hopeless case, totally lame."

"I don't think you're lame, Polly. I think you're kind and considerate, and most of the time you let Christian have his way because you could care less about status and material possessions. They're not important to you, so you let him go chasing his ambitions and collecting his toys."

Polly sighed. "It's skirt he chases most, and it's humiliating."

Annie wagged her finger. "He's the one who looks bad, not you. I hate that he killed your dream of performing."

"I let him do it, Mom." Polly voiced the hard truth. She'd played a big part in giving up her independence. Suddenly, she jumped up from the table. "Damn! I forgot to call Jay." She'd told Danelle all about the opportunity to help choreograph *Chicago* for StepWorks. "Do it," her friend had advised. "You need to keep busy with things that lift your spirits, while you eat the crap sandwich that is divorce."

Jay's phone rang and rang, before he finally answered it. "Hi, Polly. I didn't know if you'd call."

"Sorry, Jay, it's been hectic. Listen, if it's not too late, I'd like to take you up on your offer to help with auditions, rehearsals, and anything else you might need for the production."

"That's great. When I didn't hear from you yesterday, I was all set to ring other candidates. I'm glad you've decided to do it. You're my first pick for the job."

"Great!" Polly said, relieved she hadn't blown her chance and still had the gig. "What time do you want me there tomorrow for auditions?"

"Does 10:00 a.m. work?"

"Works fine. See you then." As she hung up, another call came in. It was Marcus. "Polly, do you mind coming down to the bar?" he asked all matter-of-fact. "I just had an interesting exchange with your husband."

***

An hour later, Polly was sitting next to Marcus in the Oasis. Thankfully, the place was quiet, in the lull after lunch and before the rush at quitting time. She said again how sorry she was that Christian had confronted him at work, and he waved it off. "Don't be sorry, it's not your fault."

She frowned. "Tell me again what he said." Marcus had already patiently recounted the episode, but Polly was so stressed that his words had somehow slipped around in her brain, making it hard for her to keep the story straight. He went over it again. "He came in while I was tending bar and beckoned me over. I'd seen him with Chrissy a few times, but I didn't know who he was, so I thought he'd just popped in for a drink. As I approached, he crooked his finger like this." Marcus bent his index finger in a beckoning motion.

"When I leaned over the bar, he grabbed my T-shirt, got in my ear, and hissed, 'Stay away from my wife.' Then he turned around and walked out. Since you're the only married woman I've enjoyed a thoroughly spectacular kiss with, I assumed you were the wife he was warning me to stay away from, so I called you."

"You didn't follow him?"

"No." Marcus shook his head firmly. "I thought it was best to let him cool off, and I didn't want to make a scene in front of the customers. Besides, if you were my girl, I'd run any guy who touched you out of town, so I can't say I blame him for being upset."

Polly momentarily thrilled at Marcus thinking of her as "my girl". Of course, it would be easier to believe he was pining for her if Chrissy Reynolds hadn't made it into his bed in record time. She checked herself. *I'm being unfair. I'm the one who turned him down, and some guys try to forget one girl by bedding another. I'm bringing drama to his place of work. First, I hit his truck, and now my idiot husband shows up to make a scene.* She was furious at Christian for losing his cool just because she'd exchanged a solitary kiss with Marcus, fully clothed, while jammed into the front seat of a Subaru, when he'd likely slept his way across the county. "Christian's got a nerve," she said.

"Why's he got a nerve?" Marcus cocked his head, inviting her to unload.

"I foolishly believed," Polly said, "that when we exchanged marriage vows, we both meant the part about forsaking all others. I started the week on a mission to count how many women my husband has cheated with. By the end of day two, I found out his conquests include my best friend, my wedding planner, my bookkeeper, and some woman in his office building, and I'm barely getting started." Polly didn't want to name Chrissy Reynolds of black corset fame as Christian's latest mistress. There was only so much ick she could stomach in one conversation. "I'm now taking a break from counting his floozies to get on with moving out and salvaging what's left of my dignity."

"I'm sorry." Marcus shook his head and she saw his genuine concern. "He must be crazy to step out on you." He leant down and gently kissed her lips. Polly looked around. No one was watching. So what if they were? "I hope Christian doesn't come here again," she said, but Marcus just shrugged. "Fine if he does. I'll handle him. Can't say I think too much of a man who runs around on his wife, especially when she's such a prize." Polly noticed a flash of anger in his eyes. It suggested more was bothering him than just today's fracas with Christian.

"I have to go. I'm starting a job tomorrow as a stand-in choreographer for StepWork's revival of *Chicago*, and I have to prep for auditions."

Marcus looked impressed. "Hey, wasn't that the show you starred in?"

"It was, once upon a time," Polly said, as she headed for the door.

Marcus stood for a while, thinking about Christian. The bar manager had noticed him a few times over the last few months, when he'd come in with Chrissy and sat pawing her in the corner. He'd been surprised when the guy had showed up today and announced himself as Polly's husband. What a creep. He thought about Chrissy and her stupid mind games. Did she really think that flirting with other guys and letting them low-key grope her in his bar was going to make him want her? Probably, seeing as she thought sneaking into his apartment and draping herself half-naked across his bed would turn him on. The woman had no class.

When he had finally arrived home on Friday night and caught sight of a figure in his bedroom, out of the corner of his eye, he had hoped it was Polly. Maybe she had come by to see him and was resting on his bed till he got back. But when he turned, he saw it was Chrissy, spread out like a hooker and holding a bottle of bourbon. "What are you doing here?" he'd asked sharply, startled to find her posing on his bed.

"I came to see you," Chrissy purred. "I thought I'd welcome you home with a drink and a…" she looked down at her body in the corset. Marcus followed her gaze and couldn't deny that what he saw was beautiful, but he wasn't tempted. Chrissy was putting herself out there in a way that disrespected them both. She might not know it, but she was inviting his out-and-out rejection. Too much of a gentleman to embarrass a woman who had already done enough to embarrass herself, he summoned his tact. "That's very thoughtful of you, but I prefer that guests wait for an invitation before they show up. Maybe it's the Southern boy in me." He was reluctant to humiliate the seductress for her crude come-on, but he did want to make himself clear. Nothing had changed. He still wasn't interested in having sex with her. He saw a flicker of embarrassment move across her face, as she sat up on the bed and tried to play off his rebuff. "Okay then, I will be sure to call next time and make sure you're at home for guests."

Marcus forced a smile. "I've had a long drive back from Kentucky. I have to grab a shower and help out downstairs with the rush in the bar. I hope you don't mind letting yourself out." As he headed for the shower to wash away the grime of the day, he made a mental note to tell the bar staff that they should close his apartment door tight whenever they came up to collect supplies.

CHAPTER 12: AUDITIONS

Polly faced rows of auditioning dancers who had lined up in the rehearsal room to try out for lead or ensemble roles in the StepWork's revival of *Chicago*. She recognized quite a few pros among the throng of amateurs who watched attentively as she demonstrated signature elements of Bob Fosse's acclaimed choreography. Polly explained how Fosse, an accomplished dancer himself, had borrowed extensively from the burlesque shows where he began his career. She showed the dancers how to execute hip rolls, and lift the hip while elongating the leg. She stretched out her arms in the iconic sunburst movement, and demonstrated the broken-doll, hands swinging from limp wrists. She explained in detail how to isolate different parts of the body—head, shoulders, arms, hands, hips, legs, feet, in precise, well-defined moves that gave Fosse's choreography its unmistakable style.

As Polly and Jay worked through hours of auditions, they looked for accomplished dancers who had honed their craft and could quickly master the routines to perform at a high level with energy and charisma. Next, they narrowed down candidates for call-backs, scrutinizing dancers and discussing which ones could take on lead roles as Velma

Kelly, Roxie Hart, Billy Flynn, Matron Mama Wharton, and Amos Hart.

Polly lost herself in the work, explaining dance sequences, reviewing photos and resumés with Jay, selecting the best dancers and dismissing the weak ones. It wasn't easy telling young hopefuls that they were cut, but Polly knew all about rejection and how it drove determined dancers, the serious ones, to try harder and do better. The day flew by, and when it was time to stop, she felt simultaneously exhausted and energized. Not since her days as a performer had she been so engaged and happy that when the day's work ended, she was left feeling spent but wanting more. Immersed in the music and teaching, she'd had no time to worry about the mess her life was in. Each time she glanced at her phone, she noticed the deluge of calls and texts pouring in from Chris, but she continued to ignore them. He had turned up at her parent's the night before, only to be turned away by her dad. And today at lunch, Maria had called to say Christian had barged into the studio, demanding to know where his wife was, unaware that she was off helping Jay hold auditions.

As she left the studio, Polly knew she couldn't put off seeing Christian for too much longer. Sooner or later she'd have to face the music. She felt stronger and more resolute in her decision to leave him, but she still didn't relish the confrontation she knew was brewing. Right on cue, her phone rang again, signaling another of Christian's incessant calls, and this time Polly picked up. His manner was soft and persuasive. On thin ice, he was too shrewd to explode with the rage Polly knew bubbled below his surface calm.

"I have to see you, Polly," he began before she'd barely said hello. "You have to give me a chance to explain. It's not what you think."

"You have no idea what I know and what I think, Christian," Polly pushed back. It wasn't like her to be so forceful. He was taken aback and started his wheedling. "Polly, we haven't spoken in over a week. I was worried when you didn't pick up."

"You couldn't be bothered to call me for the first two days of your trip. I'm sure you had your hands full with other women." She let her disgust at him seep into her voice.

"What's got into you, Pol?" Christian utilized the shocked and hurt tone he trotted out whenever she tried to pin him down about his bad behavior. "I know you've been talking to that Chrissy woman, but trust me, you can't go by anything she says. She's been harassing me."

"Christian, stop it! Your lying and manipulation are only making it worse."

There was another long pause before he said, "Will you at least meet me for a drink tonight?" Knowing she couldn't stall him any longer, Polly felt suddenly drained by her long day and her husband's harassment and manipulations. "Okay, where?"

"How about that Mexican place, Tres Caballeros, at half past seven?"

"Fine." She hung up, and as she headed to her parents' house to freshen up before their summit, she had to shake her head. Christian had scheduled their meeting for after his workout. Even the threat of his marriage collapsing wasn't enough to get him to switch up his routine and ditch the gym. She pictured the smug look on his face as he pressed weights, entirely convinced that he could get his wayward wife back in line.

***

At 7:45 p.m., Polly was nursing a margarita at Tres Caballeros when Christian sauntered in. His wet hair was combed back after his shower; his strong, lean but muscular body pumped up after his workout, and on show in a tight designer T-shirt. He saw her sitting at a high-top and strode briskly over with a frown. Polly felt nervous and then immediately checked herself. He was the one who should be nervous. Stopping briefly to order a drink from a passing waitress, Christian approached and sat down. He looked at her and lifted an eyebrow. "Well?"

"Well, what?" She stirred her drink with the small, plastic straw.

"Who's this guy you've been seeing?" Christian managed a look that somehow blended hurt and indignation with patient resolve.

"You have got to be kidding me!" Polly scoffed. "You've been screwing your way across New York and you're accusing me?"

"I went to see the guy at the shitty bar where he works and told him to stay away from you. I can't believe it, Pol. I've worked hard to make a good life for us and you throw it away with some bartender." Christian shook his head with a somber look and then, noticing the waitress, he took his beer from her with a dazzling smile. Polly looked on. He really was good; determined to put her on the defensive over some random kiss, while totally ignoring his own catting about. For a minute, she was thrown off, almost ready to explain away the smooch with Marcus, but then common sense struck. "Christian, I don't know what you've heard, but I am not seeing anyone. We both know you've been cheating on me. You either start explaining yourself right now, or I stand up and walk out, and you won't hear from me until divorce papers land on your mat."

Christian took a swig from his beer bottle, eyes narrowed, trying to buy time. "Okay," he said finally, "we can talk about bar boy later. What's got you so spun up?"

"I had drinks with Chrissy Reynolds. She told me about all the interesting places the two of you have sex." She wanted to sound unmoved, but the hurt was still there, lodged in her throat, threatening to make her cry.

"Oh, Polly." Christian sighed. Leaning back, he laid his outstretched arms loosely on the table, palms up. Effecting a relaxed pose to cool things down, he was exerting his uncanny ability to influence and almost hypnotize. Polly could picture him in meetings around scores of conference room tables, maneuvering to get his way over hard-core opponents and negotiators. *Don't listen to him*, she told herself. *Just sit back and watch.* He shifted in his chair, a little self-conscious under her gaze. He was used to her buying whatever line of bullshit he fed her, and not coolly appraising him like she was now.

"Chrissy Reynolds works in my building," he said. "She comes on to all the good-looking guys. We joke about it. I was flattered. I had drinks with her a few times. Nothing came of it." He took another swig of beer. *Clever,* Polly thought. *He can't deny going to the Oasis with Chrissy, because they were seen there together, so he's playing the old "he said, she said" game, like I knew he would.* Polly held up her cell phone. "Chrissy and I are on pretty good terms. Why don't I have her come join us, so she can tell us what she remembers about your affair."

"Polly, if you want to invite Chrissy Reynolds to come down here and vomit lies all over our marriage, go ahead." Christian defied her with a steely look.

"Let's stop playing games, Christian," she snapped. "I know exactly what you were up to with Chrissy. I know she dumped you because she's bored with you." She saw him flinch. "I know about Danelle, and the wedding planner, and the bookkeeper, and who knows how many other women. You're the one who has vomited all over our marriage with your putrid behavior." She wanted to lower her eyes to fight off the upset that was rising from her stomach, but she didn't.

"Polly, I know we have put off having a baby and maybe that was a bad idea..."

"I don't want a baby with you." Polly cut him off, and for the first time he looked off balance. "Hell, Christian, that is the very last thing I want."

Undeterred, he tried another tack. "Maybe it was a mistake to stop performing. You've been grumpy since you gave it up. There might be a way to combine dancing and teaching. I think we can work it out."

"I think we can work it out." His words sounded like a bell that took Polly back to their first summer together, when he'd introduced a subtle threat into their relationship. She'd insisted that she was going to Europe, and he'd implied that if she went, they might not be able to work things out, that she could lose him. He'd been manipulating her ever since, hoodwinking her, and leading her around by her nose. And she'd let him do it. She downed what was left of her margarita and stood up. "Christian, you're a liar and a cheat. The worst day of my life was the day you walked into it. Today is the day that I walk out of our marriage and your life for good. Nothing you can say or do will change my mind." She watched the effect her words had on her perplexed husband. In six years, this was the first time she had refused to play along, the first time she knew how to, and had the will to do it.

"Polly, I love you," Christian said, his voice shaking a little with apprehension, fear even. "I know I have made some mistakes. I'm sorry. I'm going to do everything I can to fix things and make you happy. You tell me what you need and we'll make it happen."

"This is not a negotiation to win some cornflakes account, Christian. I'm not some ticked-off client you can appease with a few hollow promises and cheap goodies. You've made a mockery of our wedding vows, and you've betrayed me in ways that guarantee I will never, for as long as I live, forgive you." For the first time ever, Polly knew she'd broken the spell and claimed the upper hand. She turned to go.

"Polly, people saw you making out with that bar manager in the parking lot," Christian said, his voice suddenly cold and threatening. "If anyone brings an adultery case, it will be me. I have the proof. Any woman who says I slept with her is lying."

"Christian," Polly said, "for someone who thinks he's so smart, you are as dumb as a box of rocks. Chrissy Reynolds' phone is stuffed with text messages and obscene suggestions and admissions from you."

"Just words, Polly. Just a silly game of flirtation. You have no proof. It's her word against mine."

"Whatever." Polly waved her hand to dismiss the liar and his lies.

"I'm changing the locks on the townhouse and you won't get a penny in the divorce," he threatened, his voice suddenly thick with malice.

"Do your worst." Polly strode out of the bar. Christian's audition to keep the role of her husband had been an abysmal failure.

CHAPTER 13: ESCAPE

"Are you sure it was Christian who did it?" Annie said as she drove her daughter to StepWorks for day two of auditions.

"I'm sure," Polly said, still feeling slightly numb from the shock of walking out of her parent's front door earlier that morning to discover all four tires on her Subaru had been slashed. Since the car was undrivable, her mother had scrambled to take her to work, reassuring her stunned daughter that her dad would sort the tires out later.

"Why would Christian do such a thing?" Annie asked.

Polly rolled her eyes. "Because he's a psycho, Mom. I think deep down, I knew all along that if I didn't comply, he was capable of being unreasonable, threatening even. It was just never in my nature to challenge him. I went along in a daze with whatever he wanted."

"Why? Because you were afraid of him?" Annie sounded alarmed. "Your father and I..."

Polly interrupted before she could finish. "I wasn't afraid, Mom. I was just complacent, going along to get along. For so long, I believed Christian was the best thing that ever happened to me. It was easier not to question him, not to resist him. I thought he was smarter than me, more ambitious, more successful. I let him take the lead."

Annie frowned and went quiet, aware that her daughter was on overload. Polly pressed herself into the passenger seat and thought about Christian's vicious behavior. Last night, she had come home exhausted after her long, stressful day, grabbed soup for dinner, and fallen into bed. Meanwhile, her husband was so enraged after their confrontation that he had waited until her parent's house was in darkness and then slashed her tires. Not one or two tires but all four of them. There was likely video evidence of the crime somewhere on a neighbor's security camera, although Christian was cunning. He'd probably parked at some distance and disguised his appearance. Polly had spent the last two weeks unearthing her husband's sickening sexual escapades, but this malicious act was beyond what she had believed he was capable of. Cheating is one thing. Plenty of married people do that, but slashing tires? That really put him in the box marked "lunatic."

Polly looked back on their time together. She recalled fragments of events that now, with hindsight, seemed sinister. Christian always liked to dictate what she wore, and for the most part, she humored him. He had excellent taste, and she almost always felt sexy and attractive in the clothes he picked out for her. But now and then, she'd go on a shopping spree by herself and come back with clothes that Christian didn't like. Strangely, after a little while, this clothing always seemed to disappear. She'd somehow never put it together that the only outfits that ever went missing were the ones Christian didn't like.

Worse still, she remembered how a couple of years back, when Christian was traveling so much for business, she'd adopted a cat she'd called Millie to keep her company. Even though she'd stepped up the vacuuming and dusting to keep the house spotless, Christian still complained that the cat was ruining their home. After a few months, Millie disappeared. "She probably ran away," Christian had said. Crushed, Polly spent days walking the neighborhood and putting up flyers, as she hunted for the missing kitty. When Millie never came back, she considered getting another cat, but then thought better of it. She loved having a pet, but was it really worth all the hassle with Christian? *What happened to my clothes? What happened to my cat?* she wondered now as she sat beside Annie in the passenger seat. After seeing Christian's spiteful nature on full display, it was easy to imagine him tossing her clothes in a dumpster, and dropping her cat off at a shelter, or worse. She shuddered.

Annie saw the worry on her face. "Don't spare that man another thought, Polly. Pretty soon, he's going to be out of our lives for good."

***

Like day one, day two of auditions flew by. Danelle had called it right. The work lifted Polly's spirits and distracted her from what her friend had aptly described as the crap sandwich that is divorce. Polly couldn't even begin to think about starting legal proceedings. For now, she just wanted to get her belongings out of the townhouse and extricate herself from Christian's web of lies and bully tactics. She'd deal with divorce later. "He can have everything, I don't care," Polly had told her parents when they'd discussed divorce the night before. She was drained and couldn't imagine fighting Christian for marital assets. "Over my dead body," Annie argued. And Polly knew her mother meant business. Under state law, Christian might get to keep most of the money he'd earned throughout the marriage, but Polly knew her family would help her fight for what was fair and rightly hers.

With auditions done and a great slate of dancers selected, Polly was packing up her laptop and belongings when Marcus rang again. Polly perked up. Obviously, getting involved with him, or even just being in touch, was a big mistake. But thinking of him filled her with pleasure, and gave her a case of the "what ifs." What if I could be rid of

Christian and start fresh with Marcus? What if I get to share a bed with this exciting, new lover? How would life be with a man who operated with so much character and integrity? A man she could bare her soul to, or just kick back and enjoy life with. But just as loud as the "what ifs" in Polly's head were two other words— fear and doubt. She had chosen badly when she picked Christian. She didn't want to make the same mistake twice and miss important clues about Marcus because she was too busy putting him on a pedestal. She had seen Chrissy in his bed with her own two eyes. What if Marcus, like Christian, was too good looking to stay faithful to one woman? If she'd learned one thing, it was that good-looking men were trouble. Even if they intended to be good, too much temptation made them bad. Polly couldn't trust herself to make good decisions, and the Chrissy Reynolds' debacle made her think trusting Marcus might be a bad decision. She picked up his call. "Sorry to bother you again," he said, "but your husband was in here again last night to say he would be naming me in divorce proceedings for having an affair with his wife."

Polly closed her eyes. Was there no end to the mortification? "I'm so sorry, Marcus. What did you do?"

"This time I had no choice, I had to throw him out. The bar was full and he was making a scene."

"That's fine," Polly said. "I mean it's not fine, it's understandable that you threw him out. Did he hurt you?"

Marcus laughed. "Polly, your husband is a big talker and an even bigger coward. Aside from yelling, jabbing his finger in my chest, making threats and a big ruckus, he didn't have the stones to try anything. I came around the bar, grabbed his arm, and ejected that chicken shit from the building." Polly was quiet, trying to picture the latest mayhem Christian had instigated.

"I think it might be a good idea for you to come down here, so you can tell me what's going on," Marcus said.

"I'd like to, but I don't' have a car. When I told him I was leaving him last night, Christian slashed all four of my tires, while my car was parked outside my parents' house."

"That S-O-B! Did you call the police?"

"It happened while we were asleep. I'm sure it was him, but I can't prove it, unless we go looking through the neighbors' security video."

"Polly, let me pick you up and take you to dinner." He sounded protective.

"I don't want to cause any more trouble for you."

"It's no trouble. You need a break, and excuse me, but that asshole you're married to needs to know he can't bully you. The guy's a paper tiger. He folds the minute someone his own size puts him in his place."

***

Later that evening, Polly carried the leftovers from their dinner at a nearby Chinese restaurant and followed Marcus up the stairs to his apartment. The food was delicious, but she'd only picked at her dumplings and lo mein noodles, too unsettled to eat. "Let's get out of here and go back to my place where it's quiet," Marcus said, calling for the check. It was clear he had no ulterior motives. They could talk more comfortably in the quiet of his apartment. This visit, she noticed his front door was tightly shut and locked. He let them in and put the leftovers away. "I'm having a bourbon, want one?" She nodded. They sat together on his couch, sipping the smokey liquor, letting the drink and the stillness relax them as jazz played softly in the background.

At dinner, Polly had studied Marcus's physical appearance and everything she saw turned her on. His hands as he served her and himself. The way his brown hair curled softly in the nape of his neck. The definition of his strong arms through the fabric of his shirt. Now that they were alone, she found herself irresistibly attracted to him. Curled up at one end of the couch, her knees pulled up to her chin, she studied him, as he sat at the other end, his long legs stretched out, his feet resting on an ottoman. She glanced at the bulge in his jeans and thought of how she had furtively touched its hardness on the evening he had kissed her. She wanted to touch him there now, arouse him, and discover what he would do to her when he was overtaken by lust. Would he be gentle and take his time, lingering over the act of making love, touching her in every possible place? Or would he take her in an uncontrollable rush? However it happened, Polly wanted it. The sensation between her legs was spreading and driving her to reach out for the gorgeous man, to stroke him, kiss him, and turn him loose on her body.

Marcus swirled the ice in his glass until it made a tinkling sound. He took a sip of the amber liquid and turned to look at Polly. "I have to make another trip to Kentucky tomorrow," he said quietly. "The last time I was there, I had a brief meeting with my father that did not end well."

"What happened?" Polly asked, distracted from her fantasies by his serious tone.

"Well, it's a long story for another time, but I've decided I need to go back for a do-over. I left in anger with too much unfinished business."

"Oh," Polly said, looking down and feeling vaguely vulnerable, just like she had the last time he'd left town. "I'll miss you. That must sound strange because we hardly know each other, but I like knowing you're around."

Marcus took his feet off the ottoman, sat up straight, and turned to face her. "Why don't you come with me? It might be good to get away until things cool off a little."

"I have work," Polly said. Inside, she was jumping at the idea of taking a road trip with him, but common sense told her it was a bad idea. She couldn't run away from the mess she was in. And hanging out with Marcus, no matter how innocent, only gave proof to Christian's claim that she was the one who was the adulterer and Marcus was her lover. *Why do I care?* she thought. But she did care. She was sick of Christian twisting the truth to meet his selfish ends. She didn't want to play into his hands.

"It's the weekend," Marcus coaxed. "I can have you back by Tuesday. Could your partner cover your classes for you?"

"No." Polly shook her head. "I skipped two days this week to help Jay audition and pushed so much to next week. Maria and I are both slammed."

"I'm sure your students will understand if you take a couple of days off. You're going through so much right now." His tone was gentle, respectful.

Polly felt a headache coming on. She pulled the tie from her ponytail and shook her long, dark hair loose. She saw Marcus stare at her with a hungry look in his eyes. "You look so sexy when you do that," he said, as she looked down and fumbled with the elastic tie.

"Look, Polly," he took her hand, "I'm not trying to pressure you. I'm leaving after breakfast tomorrow, after I've organized work. Why don't you stay here tonight? You can sleep in my bed and I'll take the couch. In the morning, I can drop you off at home, or you can come with me to Kentucky, whatever you decide. If you come, you'll have the weekend to sort out next week's schedule. And I'm telling you, nothing restores well-being like hanging out in the Kentucky Blue Grass Region."

"Okay," Polly said, her mind suddenly made up. "I don't need to sleep on it. I'll come with you. I think it's a good idea to skip town for a bit." His face widened with a smile, as the lines crinkled around his gorgeous blue eyes. *Damn, even his laugh lines are sexy,* she thought, and then she realized she wasn't packed for a trip. "I only have these workout clothes and some street clothes in my backpack, and I don't want to go back to the townhouse or my parents to pick my things up." She was growing allergic to the idea of going anywhere that she might run into Christian.

"I have a spare toothbrush and toiletries you can have." Marcus sounded like a kid planning an adventure. "We can stop off tomorrow and shop for a few things for you. And you can borrow gear from my mom, if you want to ride or explore the stables while we're there."

"Is that where we're going, to your mom's?" Polly asked.

"Yes, we'll use her place as a base, but I do have to go to Turner-Bell Estate to see Dad and Dawson. I'm not sure it's a good idea to take you with me, things being the way they are, but we can decide once we're down there." Polly nodded. "Look it's getting late," he said, "and you look tired. Beautiful but tired. Why don't you wash up for bed. I can give you a T-shirt and pajama pants to wear. The bathroom is through there, and there is a new toothbrush in the cabinet you can use."

Marcus rose to get the things she needed and Polly stood up. She took his hand and squeezed it. He pushed her hair aside and bent to kiss her, and just as it had before, his kiss ignited the passion between them. He pressed his mouth to hers and lifted his hand to caress her breasts that Polly had been yearning for him to touch, as she let out a moan. The kiss went on and on, as though they each had the same idea, to draw it out and excite one another to a point where her longing for him to penetrate her was exquisitely unbearable. Still upright and fully clothed, Marcus pressed his hardness into her groin, and she arched her back, rubbing herself against him. They kissed for the longest time in a state of unbridled but unconsummated passion until finally, Marcus pulled himself away. "I want you," he said, "but I want it to happen at a different time, in a different way, in a different place." He tilted her chin, and Polly looked at him with eyes that were half closed and unfocused from the desire that was radiating through her being. She nodded her head, and Marcus whispered in her ear. "I want the first time I make love to you to be perfect and something you will remember for the rest of your life." He took her by the hand and led her toward the bedroom. "Why don't you wash up before me, beauty, and then get some sleep."

***

An hour later, sitting on Marcus's bed, Polly closed her

laptop. She had texted Maria and arranged to transfer several classes to her partner's schedule. For the few remaining appointments, she emailed her students to let them know she would be out of town due to a family emergency. She texted back and forth with her mom, explaining that she was off to see a friend for the weekend.

With her schedule sorted out, Polly felt like things were somewhat under control, at least for the next few days. She looked around the bedroom at the simple but tasteful furniture, the family photos, and memorabilia. It was neat, clothes put away, bed made. The last time she had peeked inside this room, she had seen Chrissy posed on the bed and ready for sex. She flinched at the memory. She looked down at the oversized pants and tee Marcus had given her, a far cry from the sexy corset that had pushed Chrissy's breasts sky high. She lightly touched her own breasts. They were ample and full. Still aroused from earlier, she put her hand between her thighs and then pulled it away. There was something to be said for waiting.

Polly thought back to that long-ago summer's day in Callahan's Bar when Christian had followed her into the restroom and taken her so hungrily, putting sex at the center of their relationship. She couldn't lie, the sex with Chris had been amazing, but she saw now how it lacked tenderness and true intimacy. It was greedy and animalistic. It didn't arise from closeness and sharing. Chris objectified her. He studied her body parts that turned him on. He moaned at the sight of her breasts, her legs, her tight stomach, and musky wetness when she was aroused, but he didn't know anything about her innermost thoughts, hopes and fears. Of course they talked about mundane things, but her husband never troubled himself to know what she contemplated in the deepest part of her being. And in the same way, Polly realized, Christian had always been unknowable to her. She knew all the superficial things about him—his ambitions, his likes and dislikes, but she hadn't penetrated his core. When they went out with his friends, she sensed they knew a different Chris, one that he showed to them but not to her. Sitting in Marcus's bed, Polly acknowledged that she really knew no more about her husband today than she had on that first date at Callahan's. When Christian had closed the door of the restroom to capture her sexually, he had shut and locked another kind of door that led to the intimacy she now craved with a different man, a better man.

She turned off the light and lay in the dark. Her body ached for Marcus. She wanted to tip toe into the living room where he slept, find his mouth, and launch more desperate arousal, but something inside her thrilled at the idea that, if she waited, she would eventually connect with the whole man. And then she remembered again that Marcus had taken Chrissy in this very bed. She imagined them together, the blonde's legs wrapped tightly around his taut body, pulling him in until he penetrated her. Tears spilled from the corners of her eyes and ran down her cheeks. Sex was dangerous. She hungered for Marcus. She wanted to lie under him and receive the same pleasure that Chrissy had, but she was afraid. She loved the man who had so tenderly cared for her tonight, but she feared the part of him that had taken Chrissy with the same lust that Christian had. The smell, and look, and taste of her rival had pulled both of the men in Polly's life into Chrissy's orbit and into her body. And that fact filled her with worry.

CHAPTER 14: ROAD TRIP

"Morning, beautiful," Marcus whispered in Polly's ear as she slept. She opened her eyes to see him holding fresh coffee and a breakfast wrap.

"Bar work's all done," he announced. "Shelves are well stocked and the staff schedule is nailed down."

Polly sat up and stretched, feeling well rested. Through the curtains, she saw that a beautiful summer's morning had dawned bright and clear. She took the breakfast Marcus proffered with a smile. "Can you be ready in forty minutes or so?" he inquired. "It's a long drive and I want to get a jump on traffic."

Polly had showered the night before, casting off her workout gear. This morning, she pulled on the jeans, T-shirt, and hoodie she kept in her backpack. By ten o'clock, the pair were buckled into the pick-up and grinning like two adventurers ready for their road trip. Marcus stopped briefly at a drive-thru for more coffee, then cranked up the radio's classic rock channel and hit the highway. Polly was overtaken by a feeling of freedom and excitement. At least for this weekend, she could escape Christian, her impending divorce, and the prison her life had become. She would give herself over to fun and relaxation, and maybe even romance with the leggy Kentucky horse guy, who looked psyched to have her along for the ride.

Come mid-afternoon, as they traversed Ohio, they pulled off the highway and followed signs to a nearby mall. Climbing out of the truck, they stretched, made their way to the mall's food court, and grabbed a quick lunch. Once they were done, Marcus tugged enthusiastically on Polly's hand. "Come on, I want to buy you something pretty to wear. Is that alright?" She hesitated. Years of Christian picking out her clothes, as just another way to exert control over her, had left a nasty taste in her mouth. But one look at Marcus told her he was driven by the simple desire to please her, so she nodded with a shy smile.

The pair walked arm-in-arm through the mall, headed for a high-end department store. Standing before a well-curated rack of summer dresses, Marcus squinted and turned to Polly with a confused look, clearly unschooled in the gentle art of picking out women's clothes. "See anything you like?" Polly flicked through the racks, selecting an array of dresses to try on, as well as an assortment of tops and a pair of linen pants. For thirty minutes, she modeled the outfits for Marcus, as he patiently waited outside the changing rooms, his face lighting up every time she emerged in a new dress. "I love it. Get it," he insisted, as she strutted and twirled in a succession of outfits that showcased her spectacular figure. "I can't get it all." Polly laughed.

"Why not?" Marcus argued. "It all looks great on you."

Polly picked out the dress she liked best. Rose colored, it was worn off the shoulders with a fitted bodice and a long, fluted skirt. It made her feel girlish and feminine. She also settled on the comfortable cream linen pants that tied with a drawstring; a boxy, blue cotton top; a few T-shirts, and a pair of strappy sandals. Marcus paid with his credit card, taking the bag of clothes that were swaddled in tissue. "Thank you." Polly kissed his cheek and he grinned.

"Thank you, lovely lady."

Back on the road, Polly looked out at the passing

landscape and couldn't remember the last time she had felt so alive and optimistic. It was late evening and dark, as Marcus drove up the long driveway, past the paddocks and the horses, to park outside his mom and Mac's farmhouse. In the stables, the horses were quiet after a long day carrying riders, galloping across the fields, and slow walking the trails.

"Mom, Mac, this is Polly." Marcus didn't so much introduce the woman he was falling in love with, as he presented her like a jewel to his parents. Polly reached out her hand, but both Jenny and Mac pulled her in for a hug. Early risers, they had waited up past their bedtime to welcome Marcus and the first woman he had brought home since moving out of state. Jenny didn't know what this dark-haired, graceful beauty meant to her son, but she did know that right when Polly had come into his life, Marcus had decided to set aside bitterness and entertain a long hoped-for reconciliation with his father. She prayed this signaled his return to Turner-Bell Estate and the business he had been born to run.

Jenny showed Polly to a guest bedroom, and set down the chamomile tea she had made her on the antique bedside table. Exhausted from the long travel day, Polly showered and fell into bed, climbing between the crisp white sheets that smelled of lavender.

***

Polly awoke early the next morning, well-rested. From outside, she could hear the sound of muffled voices and the clomping of horses' hooves on the driveway, as Mac mucked out the stables. She breathed in the fresh country air that wafted through the bedroom's open window. As she made her way downstairs for breakfast, she passed through the hall that led to the kitchen and suddenly stopped short when she heard Marcus speaking with his mother. "You didn't tell me she was married," Jenny said, a sharp note of surprise in her voice. Polly stayed in the hallway and listened. She didn't want to eavesdrop, but she was unsure about how to walk in on mother and son and interrupt a conversation that seemed to be about her.

"She's divorcing, Mom." Marcus sounded patient but firm, like a grown man who makes his own decisions, although it was clear to Polly that his mother's opinion carried a lot of weight.

"Wouldn't it be a better idea to wait until she extricates herself from a bad situation so you don't drag all that drama into your life?" Jenny asked.

"I recall that you didn't necessarily wait to extricate yourself before taking up with Mac," Marcus said, immediately regretting the dig. "I'm sorry, Mom. That was out of line."

Polly could feel the strained silence that followed. Eventually, Jenny spoke up. "It's okay if you think I am a hypocrite, Marcus. I'm not a paragon of virtue. I'm simply a mother who loves you and wants the best for you."

"Mom, I'm sorry. That was an unkind and unfair thing to say. I just have a lot of things to work out, and I'm trying to keep my bearings. Polly makes me happy. She's the only bright spot at the moment."

Trapped in the hallway, Polly decided she couldn't loiter much longer, while a three-act play unfolded in the kitchen. She got it. Jenny was concerned about her son getting involved with a woman whose husband was bad news. What mother wouldn't worry? But she'd also heard Marcus confess that she was the bright spot in his life, so that was good, seeing as she saw him as the light at the end of a long, dark tunnel. She strolled into the kitchen, trying to appear oblivious to the tense conversation underway. Marcus had wrapped his mother in a bear hug to soothe the hurt feelings he'd caused, and seeing her guest was up and about, Jenny extricated herself from his arms. "Good morning, I hope you slept well. What would you like for breakfast?" Polly pointed to a glass-covered dish. "One of those bran muffins with a little butter and jelly would be lovely." Judging by his plate, it looked like Marcus had feasted on a full breakfast of sausage, egg, home fries, and all the fixings.

After breakfast, Marcus took Polly to the stable. She watched him handle the horses with perfect ease, walking between them, stroking their long faces, and breathing into their nostrils, while he whispered gentle sounds into ears that pricked up and twitched. After she'd studied the scene for a while, she broke the silence. "You love it here."

"I do." Marcus pressed his face against the head of the huge beast he was communing with. "Do you want to go for a ride?"

She laughed. "I haven't been on a horse since I was a little girl. Broken legs are not good for a dancer's career."

"Nah, we've got you." Marcus moved toward a stall where an old and slightly pudgy mare was quietly feasting on her hay. "Old Nancy here is gonna treat you right, aren't you, Nancy?" Marcus saddled up Mister Sturdy for himself and Nancy for Polly. After fitting her with a helmet, he boosted her into the saddle, and then led her, along with his own horse, out of the stable. Outside, he mounted and turned to Polly. "We're just going to take a nice gentle walk around the property. Nothing fancy, okay?" Polly nodded from atop Nancy, who didn't so much walk as waddle, and soon relaxed into the gentle sway of the old horse's gait.

Polly looked around, taking in the orderly lines of white fencing and the beauty of the luscious landscape. When they'd walked in silence for about twenty minutes and found themselves in one of the small farm's furthest fields, Marcus dismounted and helped Polly down. They sat under the shade of a tree while the two horses, now free of riders, bowed their heads and grazed. Polly stretched out her legs and watched Marcus as he chewed on a long grass stem. He was relaxed, at ease with himself, open and transparent. Different than Christian who was somehow closed and hidden, always on the move and plotting his next coup. On their ride, Polly had mulled over what she'd heard in the kitchen. "Marcus," she said after a while. "When I came down to breakfast, I didn't mean to, but I overheard you talking to your mom. I know she can't be happy about you getting all caught up in my mess."

Marcus looked uncomfortable. "She's just being a mom. I'm thirty-five. She respects that I make my own decisions." He bit down on the grass.

"I heard you tell her that you're working a lot of things out. You know my ugly story, I think it's only fair that I know yours."

Marcus looked tentative. "It's a long story." Polly stretched out her arm and made a sweeping motion across the quiet field and the landscape beyond. "Well, it looks like we've got all day," she said.

Marcus paused for a minute to organize his thoughts before he began. "Mom's family had a sizeable horse business—Turner Farm. Dad's family also had a large concern—Bell Farm. The properties were side-by-side, so growing up, Mom knew Dad, Jock Junior, or JJ, as he was called, seeing as they lived so close and moved in the same circles. But Mom's heart always belonged to Mac Campbell. Mom and Mac were childhood sweethearts and always planned to get married. From being a kid, Mac worked for Mom's dad, my Grandpa, Winston Turner. Mac started out as a stable hand, but over the years, he gained Winston's trust and worked up to be the farm's main manager. He pulled himself up by the bootstraps and was really like a son to my grandpa. Mom was Winston's only child and heir, so grandpa leaned more and more on Mac to help her with the running of the farm." Marcus paused and took a drink from his water bottle. "Next door at Bell Farm, Jock went away to college to get a degree that would help him run the business. The summer he graduated and came home from college, Mac was away, dealing with family matters after his father died. From what I can gather, Dad swept Mom off her feet, and I guess they had a fling, because by the time Mac came back, Mom was pregnant with me. Mom didn't want to marry Jock, but the two families shot gunned it. Anyway, they liked the idea of not only merging families, but also merging farms. When Mom married Jock, Turner-Bell Estate was created, and Dad ran it. Made a good job of it, too."

"What did Mac do?" Polly asked, grasping all the complications.

"Mac and Mom continued to represent Grandpa Turner's interests in Turner-Bell. Mac was still involved, managing the Turner side of the property, even after the two farms merged and my Dad became head honcho."

"But your Mom and Mac are together now, right?"

"Yes, they are, but they weren't together back then. Mom and Mac are both people with integrity. After Mom got married, they made sure their relationship was purely professional. Growing up, Mac was like a second father to me, but whatever his feelings for Mom were, I never saw him treat her as anything other than a business associate and another man's wife. Jock on the other hand..." Marcus shook his head and threw away the mangled grass stalk, before plucking a fresh one. "If you ask anyone around here about Jock Bell the third, they'll tell you he is a breeder of championship horses, a bedder of beautiful women, and a drinker of fine bourbon."

"So, your dad had affairs?" Polly asked.

"That, my lady, is the understatement of the century," Marcus scoffed. "My father bedded everything in sight, often right under Mom's nose."

"She must have felt humiliated," Polly said, feeling her own humiliation, where it sat like a hot coal in her stomach.

Marcus shook his head. "Mom always quoted Eleanor Roosevelt. Something to the effect that no one can humiliate you without your permission. Dad was the one who looked small not Mom, and the smaller he looked, the more he cheated on her to look bigger and get a rise out of her. I think he knew she was always in love with another man, with Mac, and was never really his. She stayed in the marriage for the sake of my brother and me and the business. Turner-Bell means everything to Mom, and keeping it safe for her two sons has always been her mission."

"So, what happened? She's obviously not married to Jock anymore."

Marcus focused on a group of horses grazing in a distant field. "I lived and worked at Turner-Bell until I was twenty-five. That was the year Jock went off the rails. He was drinking more, sleeping with more women. He always ran the business at a profit, but he was making Mom's life miserable. One afternoon he came roaring back, after a drinking session with his friends at the club. One of them had made some innuendo about Mom and Mac being all cozy in the barn together. A farmhand had seen Mac with his arms around Mom, comforting her, and he put it about that Mac was bedding her on hay bales."

"Were they having an affair?" Polly asked.

"I don't know," Marcus said. "I don't think so, though I wouldn't blame them if they were driven to it at that point. Mac never stopped loving Mom. I think it broke his heart to see the way Jock treated her. He would have walked away from Turner-Bell years ago, once Jock took it over, but he stayed to watch over Mom, Grandpa Winston, and us boys."

"Wow, Mac is some guy!" Polly was starting to see where Marcus got his good character from.

"Yes, he is," Marcus agreed. "Anyway, on that fateful afternoon, I was working in the stable with Mom. We'd just finished our chores, and she was already up on her favorite horse, about to take a ride when Dad showed up. He was in a fit of rage after his drinking party at the club, where he'd heard the gossip about Mom and Mac. We tried to calm him, but he was absolutely unhinged with fury. He was screeching that Mom was a whore and only fit to screw a jumped-up farm hand."

"What did your mom do?"

"She just looked down at him, figuratively and literally. She was astride a large gelding, looking down at Dad like he was some madman, in the way of her afternoon ride. Dad grabbed her riding crop and raised it to hit her, but he somehow missed and struck her horse in the eye. The horse panicked, rose up, and threw Mom. She got caught between the horse and the stable door and he trampled her."

Polly brought her hand to her mouth. "Oh my Lord, is that why she limps?"

"Yes," Marcus said. "I watched a twelve hundred pound horse stomping my mother for what felt like an eternity, as we struggled to get him off her. The gelding broke her pelvis and back and caused horrific internal injuries." There was a long silence as Polly waited for Marcus to regain his composure. "She had numerous surgeries. They weren't sure she'd walk again. She left Dad and Turner-Bell. After the divorce, she settled for a lump sum of money that she used to buy the stables, and an ironclad agreement that ownership of Turner-Bell would, in time, be turned over to Dawson and me."

"Did she marry Mac?" Polly asked.

"No. Dad said he wouldn't agree to her terms if she remarried. He knew it would pain her to live out of wedlock with Mac but he wouldn't yield."

"You mean even after he crippled her, he still wanted to hurt her?" Polly thought that Christian was a fiend, but this guy, Jock Bell, made him look like a boy scout.

"That's right," Marcus said with a sigh. "But you know what they say? The opposite of love isn't hate, it's indifference. My mother was always indifferent to Jock because she never loved him. Jock only hated my mother so much because he loved her so madly and knew he couldn't really possess her."

"Is that why you left?" Polly asked.

"Yes. I watched my mother suffer agony, as she recovered and forced herself to walk again. She was a horsewoman and outdoors fanatic. Jock took that from her.

To this day, every step she takes is painful. My mother will always be beautiful, but my father made her old before her time. I wanted to kill Jock Bell for what he did. She begged me to stay, but I didn't feel like any kind of man living and working around Dad after what he'd done. I wanted to choke the life out of him, not sit down and discuss the price of feed with him."

"Are you ready to come back now?" Polly asked, realizing she may have met the man of her dreams right as he was about to pack up and leave town.

"Yes, I am. I love Kentucky and Turner-Bell. I never wanted to leave. If you'd ever told me back when I was twenty that I would leave this paradise for a week let alone a decade, I'd have thought you were crazy. Also, my being gone hurts Mom and Dawson. They feel like I abandoned them. Mom sacrificed so much for us to inherit our birthright, carry on her legacy, and become the fourth generation of Turners to breed horses."

Polly understood. "So, that's why the change of heart?"

"Yes, and Dad's been in ill health. I'm not gonna lie, many a time I hoped he'd die so I could come back and run the place in peace, without him and what he did hanging over me." He grimaced. "I know that sounds terrible. I bet you think I'm awful."

"I don't think you're awful." Polly rubbed his arm to soothe him and felt the firmness of his muscles. "And I don't think you really want your dad to die. I know what it's like when someone hurts you so much you never want to set eyes on them, let alone have to wake up and work with them every day."

Marcus stroked her cheek and kissed her. He rolled on top of her and pinned her body to the ground, hungrily claiming her lips, thrusting his tongue in and out of her soft, wet mouth. He put his hand inside her shirt and fondled her breast, rubbing the warm flesh in circles with his palm. Mr. Sturdy looked up momentarily to glance at the writhing bodies on the ground beneath the tree, then went right back to grazing on the sweet Kentucky blue grass.

***

Come early evening, Jenny and Mac served a picnic dinner outdoors. The table was set with a blue checked cloth, and loaded with fresh greens and salad, along with pulled pork and ribs. "I'll dance this off next week." Polly laughed. She was a little late coming down from the long shower she'd taken to recover from the make-out session. She and Marcus had abstained from having sex in an open field, but they'd come pretty close. Her hair was down, and she wore the off-the-shoulder, rose-colored dress that Marcus had gifted her. She saw his face was full of admiration when she appeared in the garden. "She's a beauty, Mac," Jenny said, as Polly took her seat at the table.

"She certainly is," Mac replied, but Polly noticed when he said this, he had taken Jenny's hand and was kissing it with the look of a man who was totally besotted with his woman. She caught Marcus looking at his parents. He caught her eye and smiled, as if to say, how's that for real love?

PENELOPE HOLT

CHAPTER 15: HOMECOMING

The next day was Sunday, and Polly dressed up in the new linen pants and blue, boxy top. She studied her face in the mirror. She looked rested and relaxed. And she'd caught a little sun. She had to admit it, new romance and getting away from all the stresses in her life had restored her beauty. The last time she'd looked this radiant had been when she was still performing, and she'd come off stage each night looking flushed, happy, and alive. Marcus knocked and put his head around the bathroom door. "May I come in?"

"Sure." Polly turned away from the mirror to face him.

"You look stunning. You're more beautiful every time I see you. What witchcraft and dark arts are you practicing, woman?" he growled in mock accusation, as he grabbed her, lifted her up, and kissed her. Polly laughed, feeling like a giddy prom queen in love with the high-school jock. It was excruciating not to give into lust and sexual abandon, but it was also exciting. Each time they kissed, it further fueled Polly's fantasies about how it would feel when Marcus was finally inside her, filling her with the hardness she'd so far only caressed through his jeans. She kept thinking about his promise, that the first time they made love would be perfect and something she'd remember forever. So far, his every touch had been memorable. Polly continually replayed in her mind how they had kissed in the parking lot outside the Oasis, then again in Marcus's apartment, and beneath the trees here at the farm. She could barely wait to consummate what, so far, they'd left half-finished.

Marcus became serious. "If you're up for it, I'd like you to come to Dad's with me. I'll need to speak privately with him, but I think having you there will help keep things calm. Okay?"

"Sure." Polly nodded and kissed him.

Ready to leave for the half-hour drive to Turner-Bell, they made their way outside, and were met with the sight of Jenny and Mac sitting in their pick-up, in the driveway, engine idling. Marcus leaned on their cab's open window. "Where are you two off to?"

"Your dad called," Jenny said. "He asked us to ride over with you to Turner-Bell." Marcus frowned and went to say something but changed his mind. Instead, he helped Polly into his truck, and they set off with Jenny and Mac following. They drove in silence for a little while, as Polly mulled over a question that had eaten away at her since she'd seen Chrissy on Marcus's bed. She felt more at ease now, and brave enough to risk questioning him. "I don't know if you know this but Christian slept with that woman Chrissy Reynolds." Marcus took his eyes off the road to give her a sympathetic look. "I thought that might be the case. They came in the bar a few times and he was pretty handsy with her. It didn't look like they were getting together to talk business."

"Is she good in bed?" Polly asked, finally able to blurt out what she'd been too afraid to ask until now.

Now when he answered, Marcus didn't take his eyes off the wheel. "I don't know, she's not my type."

Polly felt like a heavy weight had fallen from the sky and landed on her chest. He was lying to her. She had spent the last couple of weeks taking in this wonderful man's every word and move, hoping to convince herself that he was honorable, a gentleman, a man she could trust. Marcus was the complete opposite of Christian in almost every way, but in one crucial aspect, it appeared they were identical; they both screwed women and lied about it.

Polly looked out of the truck's window so Marcus wouldn't see how upset she was. She'd been convinced that when asked about Chrissy, he would come clean and brush it off as a nothing-burger. If she could just clear the air about that night, she felt certain she'd be able to move forward and give herself to him completely. Her eyes pooled with unspilled tears, as she saw her situation for what it was. Hundreds of miles from home, her life in a mess, she was once again deluding herself about romance. To boot, she was stuck in a truck with a guy she only thought she knew but really didn't, and he was taking her to a tense showdown with his no-good, cheating, wife-abusing father.

As they drove up the long driveway on the approach to the magnificent Turner-Bell Estate, Polly took in the sprawling two-story main building that was topped with three small bell towers. It looked more like a stately manse than a farm. White fenced paddocks were laid out, one after another, and a series of well-kept barns, stables, and outbuildings gave proof that a multi-million dollar business was in operation here. An expanse of perfectly manicured lawn led up to the arched portico of the house's main entrance. Marcus parked and Polly climbed out. The grandeur of the setting on such a beautiful summer's day was enough to distract her from the crushing disappointment that Marcus's lie had triggered.

Jock kissed Polly's hand when she was introduced. He was thin, frail, and like his ex-wife, he walked with a stick, but Polly could see that the urge to seduce women was still alive and well in the old dog. Once a womanizer, always a womanizer, she thought as she smiled politely. "Pleased to meet you." Dawson came bounding out of the house to hug his brother, introduce himself to Polly, and then make a beeline for Jenny and Mac, who had arrived and were parking in the driveway.

Jock had arranged for an elegant lunch to be served on the back patio. He ushered them through the opulence of the main floor, and out the French doors to the back of the property that overlooked the vast acreage of the estate. Passing through the foyer, Polly eyed massive oil paintings in gilt frames of family portraits interspersed with champion thoroughbreds. She shot Marcus a questioning look. He liked to play the humble, down-home barkeep and everyman, but Polly could see he was a child of considerable wealth. He came from a clan of savvy business people, who bet and won big on the fickle game that was high-stakes racehorse breeding. Looking around the elegant property and furnishings, she saw that the Turner-Bells were connoisseurs when it came to partaking in luxuries that the best of life had to offer.

Outdoors, a butler served a lunch of broiled salmon, salad, and roasted vegetables, with a crisp white wine. They ate in uncomfortable silence, as any attempt at small talk fizzled and died. Even if she hadn't learned the family's backstory, Polly could have guessed from the tense atmosphere that this gathering was more than a little awkward. It was clear that old wounds and past conflicts lay just below the surface. But when Dawson steered the stilted conversation onto the topic of horses, the entire group became instantly animated and seemed to set aside differences to talk about their shared passion. They barely let each other finish, as they all jumped in, talking shop and sharing gossip. They traded news on rival farms, what they knew about fillies, geldings, and stud horses, as well as records that were being broken in horse sales and siring fees.

Marcus caught Polly's eye and mouthed, "I'm sorry." She smiled and shrugged. It was easy to see that this was where he belonged. Surrounded by his family in his natural habitat, he looked more alive, energized, and, yes, handsomer, than she'd ever seen him in their brief time together. Surreptitiously, she studied Jenny and Mac, as they sat side by side. They looked at ease, like time and the tide had washed away whatever bitterness and resentment they felt toward Jock Bell, the man who had damaged their lives and almost ruined them altogether.

Finally, Jock held up his hand and the chatter died down, as the gathering turned to the patriarch who had an announcement to make. Jenny and Mac exchanged glances and joined hands. "Marcus, I want to welcome you home," Jock began. "We've missed you. I have something to say, and I wanted Dawson, your mother, and Mac to be present to hear it. And I'm delighted you have brought such a beautiful young woman to join us." He smiled at Polly. "Because, at times like this, it's a fine idea to have a witness on hand. I very much doubt folks will ever believe what is about to come out of my mouth unless it is repeated by a reliable witness or sworn to in a court of law." Dawson smiled at his father, seemingly aware of what was coming. Jock hesitated, trying to stick his courage, as everyone looked on expectantly. He caught Jenny's eye, and she nodded, as if to say, "You can do it." Then the old, stubborn reprobate took a deep breath and looked directly in their eyes as he spoke. He began to address each of the individuals around his table. "Jenny, I am sorry," he said. "I have hurt you in the worst ways. I have brought you emotional and physical pain and heartache. I am ashamed and sorry beyond measure. I ask your forgiveness, although I know I don't deserve it."

Polly saw tears glistening in Jenny's eyes "I forgive you, Jock," she said simply. Next, Jock turned to Mac. "I am sorry, Mac. You are the better man. You deserve the love of this fine lady, and it's probably high time you made an honest woman of her with no interference from me." Mac, didn't say anything, he just nodded and squeezed Jenny's hand. Jock looked now at his youngest son. "Dawson, I am sorry. Because of my despicable actions, the burden of my ill health and running the business has been on your young shoulders. When you should have been off exploring the world and having adventures, you've been toiling here, and paying the price for your father's foolish mistakes and bad behavior."

Dawson leaned forward and stroked his father's hand. This youngest Bell seemed to have the easiest time loving and forgiving the old man. Jock turned next to Marcus who was brimming with barely contained emotion. "Marcus, you are my oldest son, my pride and joy. A real man protects the women in his life and punishes those who dare hurt them. I know that I drove you away from this place that you love. I know it was self-restraint that kept you away and stopped you from ripping apart the father who hurt your mother and this family so badly. Son, please forgive me." Marcus couldn't say anything. He swallowed hard and nodded silently.

"And finally, Miss Polly," Jock turned to the stranger at his table, who was mortified to find herself at the center of attention in this unfolding family drama. "I'm sorry if I've spoiled a lovely afternoon by involving you in such a difficult and intimate scene."

"Well, I'll take a peace summit over a brawl any day," Polly said, and everyone laughed. It felt like a huge burden was rolling off every family member, and a toxic past, if not entirely put to rest, was finally set to heal.

***

Later in the afternoon, Marcus and Polly peeled away to walk the property, leaving the family to their horse talk on the patio. Still smarting from the shock of his lie, Polly reluctantly let Marcus take her hand. He entwined their fingers and brought her hand to his mouth to kiss it.

"It looks like it's settled and you're coming back here," she said after a while.

"I think so." Marcus's tone suggested that while his mind was made up, his emotions were still catching up. "Polly, I know it's a lot to ask, but would you consider coming down here to be with me?"

"And what would I do here?" Polly asked skeptically. She'd already pressed pause on her life once to live Christian's dream. Doing it all over again for another man seemed like a bad idea, especially since this new man was triggering old fears. She looked out at the expanse of acres, costly equipment, and complex of buildings that comprised Turner-Bell Estate. She had to admit that living here with Marcus seemed like it might be a dream come true, but knowing her luck in love, it could just as easily turn out to be a recipe for disaster. No, it was time to focus on herself and her career, no distractions.

Marcus noticed her somber mood and tried teasing her. "You know, there are lots of little girls down here in tutus who would love to learn how to dance from such a beautiful teacher."

"I don't really love teaching," Polly said. "I'd like to get back to performing." The two days she'd spent with Jay, running auditions for *Chicago*, had rekindled her desire to dance more and teach less, as she figured out how to make ends meet as a soon-to-be-divorced woman.

"Well, we do have a thriving cultural center and the arts down here, you know," Marcus said a little defensively. "We're not hicks. The horse scene and the Kentucky Derby make for an engaged community and lively social calendar. There are plenty of outlets for performers, and it's less cutthroat than New York, more gracious, I think."

"I don't know." Polly continued to feel uncertain about everything, especially Marcus. "We should get back."

It was almost dusk, when the two trucks pulled out of Turner-Bell's main gate to head back to Mac and Jenny's place. Before they left, Jock had insisted on a shot of bourbon for the road. "No alcohol for you," Dawson intoned, glaring at his dad. Boy, he really is old for his years, Polly thought, as she focused again on the youngest member of the Bell clan who, in many ways, appeared to be the most measured of them all. Ignoring his son's reprimand, Jock turned to Polly. "Honored guest, why don't you propose a toast?" The others held up their cut crystal rocks glasses of premium Kentucky bourbon, waiting for Polly's parting toast. "To recapturing dreams," she said, looking at Marcus, who noticed a strange look in her lovely green eyes.

CHAPTER 16: RECAPTURING DREAMS

Jay and Polly sat on metal chairs in StepWork's rehearsal room, poring over the eight-by-ten headshots spread out before them on a table. "This one shows promise," Polly said, pointing to a blonde with curly hair.

"Nope." Jay threw up his hands. "Polly, I know you don't want to hear this, but the best person to play Velma Kelly is you."

Rehearsals were about to get underway and they had been able to cast all the principle roles, except for Velma. "Come on, Jay," Polly scoffed, "there's plenty of good dancers to choose from."

Jay shook his head emphatically. "They're all second best compared to you. I really want you to take the role. You said yourself that you owed me?" His look suggested he was only half joking.

"Hey, I thought I scrubbed that debt when I jumped in to help with auditions and rehearsals," Polly shot back.

"Look, think about it overnight. If you don't agree, we'll go with curly top." Jay held up the photo of the kinky-haired blonde and scrutinized it with a disappointed look.

"She's a good dancer and she'll be wearing a wig," Polly argued. "I must confess, I don't miss wearing a steaming cap of fake hair on my head, while I high kick across the stage."

Jay poked her arm with his finger. "You loved it."

"I did love it." Polly sighed. Jay noticed there was something in her look that made him think he might still talk her into taking the role. "This one," he pointed to the photo of curly top, "will work just fine in the chorus."

***

That night, as Polly lay in the single bed in her childhood bedroom, she looked up at the ceiling and wondered how she'd got there. Her life was going backward. She was living with her parents, on the brink of divorce, with a humdrum career, and no clear plan for the future.

Marcus had packed up and left for Kentucky a few weeks earlier. He'd invited her to the Oasis for his going away party. The place had been packed to the rafters with friends and well-wishers, so she'd only stayed for one drink before whispering in Marcus's ear that she had to leave. With a forlorn look, he'd walked her out to her Subaru. Reggie had done a good job fixing the bumper and charged her next to nothing. When she'd given the mechanic her profuse thanks and handed him a credit card to swipe, he'd shrugged and said cryptically that Marcus was a great guy. Polly guessed that Marcus had paid practically the whole bill, and told Reggie to charge her just a couple hundred dollars. Marcus, always chivalrous, but sometimes a liar.

"I thought we had something special, Polly," Marcus said, as they stood once again by her car in the infamous parking lot, over two months after their first memorable clinch there.

"Bad timing, that's all," Polly argued, and when Marcus leaned in to kiss her, she pulled away. She couldn't handle his kisses and what they did to her. They sent her lusting for sex and love and dreams that she doubted could turn into reality.

What's your problem, Polly? she asked herself now in the

quiet of the cramped, cluttered bedroom that her mom used to store random boxes, a sewing machine, and supplies. She knew the answer. She'd lost her confidence. Poof, it was all gone, evaporated. Marcus had boosted her confidence, just like Christian had back when they were first dating, but look how that turned out. She never again wanted to depend on a man to feel good about herself, especially one who had the power to hurt her. She had tried to make excuses for Marcus and write off his lie about not sleeping with Chrissy. Maybe, she told herself, he was too embarrassed to admit it, or convinced that since the sex didn't matter, the best move was to sweep it under the rug. After all, Marcus didn't know lying about sex with other women was Polly's kryptonite. *Would he cheat on me if we were together?* Polly asked herself. Probably not. But that no longer mattered. The harm was done. There was something about Marcus's lie that had stopped her in her tracks and prevented her from going any further with him.

She looked over at a bulletin board on the bedroom wall that was covered with memorabilia from her youth. She focused on a photo that showed her, on a bright summer's day, with a crowd of young friends, huddling together on a bluff as they stared down at the lake below them. She remembered how all the kids in the neighborhood would stand on that bluff in their bathing suits, too afraid to jump, taunting one another to take the plunge. One by one, each of the kids worked up the courage to take the leap into the water, and then they'd splash around, trying to coax the others, who were still too chicken to jump. "It's easy, just do it," the brave ones would yell from the water. Polly had been one of the last to jump. Eventually she had psyched herself up, and when she did finally take the leap, hers had not been just any old jump. Polly had done a dancer's grand jeté off the bluff, and when she hit the water, she had felt invincible. As she stared at the photo from that faraway day, she was reminded that inside her was a fearless girl, who knew how to take a leap into the unknown. She just had to find her again.

***

The next morning, as Polly sauntered into StepWorks, Jay started laughing. Walking over to greet her, he gave her a warm hug. "You're going to do it," he said, beaming.

"I'm going to do it," Polly said, as she stood before him, sporting a dark bob, thanks to the Prince Valiant wig she had pulled out of storage and fixed on her head. In the summer heat, it was making her hot and sweaty. "I'm roasting." She laughed. "What we do for our art." And then she rotated on the spot, as she executed a series of perfectly sexy hip rolls.

When Jay announced to the company that Polly would be taking on the role of Velma Kelly in the production, they all cheered. Even curly top, who Polly had beat out for the role, clapped enthusiastically. Polly was popular with all of the dancers. Encouraging and supportive, she was always there with valuable pointers to help them punch up their performance.

***

In the weeks that followed, Polly rehearsed nonstop. She knew the role so completely, and had done it so often on stage, that in no time, she was performing at the height of her powers. "Damn, you're better than ever," Jay called out, as Polly perfected Velma Kelly's show-stopping numbers. What had originally been slated as a short local run for the musical was extended to five cities, over two months, not as big as the company's previous twenty-city tour but still impressive.

Polly was still figuring out how to make it work at Beat It, while she was away on tour. Danelle had volunteered to help. "I can drive down and teach classes a couple of days each week," she offered. "Mom will look after Louis Junior.

I need to get out of the house and back to dance. Teaching yoga is not for me." Maria liked the idea of Danelle helping out. Keeping two instructors meant that they could continue to market the business, bring in students, and keep revenue flowing.

After weeks of worry and trepidation, Polly left rehearsal one night feeling exhilarated. Her hard work was paying off, and much to her surprise, the divorce was going more smoothly than she'd expected. Danelle's prediction that Christian wouldn't want to waste money on lawyers turned out to be accurate. The couple had opted for mediation, and as a result, Christian had agreed to sell the townhouse and split the proceeds with Polly. He was sick of the place anyway and ready for something more upmarket. As long as she didn't go after alimony and he got to keep his cash, Christian was proving pretty easy to deal with. Negotiations were moving along at a good pace. For her part, Polly had agreed to let Christian keep their furniture. There was no room for it at her parents, and she would be on tour for a couple of months, with no place to store any of it. And besides, like most everything in their life together, Christian had picked out all the pieces, according to his taste. True to form, on any shopping trips to furnish their home, he'd managed to steer Polly away from what she liked and talk her into what he wanted.

For a few weeks after Marcus had left New York for Kentucky, he had texted Polly frequently. She'd stopped short of ghosting him, but she had been deliberately slow to answer, kept her replies short, and never picked up on his offers to "chat sometime". Over time, her spurned beau seemed to get the message that she had cooled toward him, and his steady stream of texts dwindled down to the occasional "Greetings from Kentucky." But at night, in her dreams, Polly relived the deeply erotic moments she had shared with the man who had captivated her and was now hundreds of miles away. She wanted to forget him, but her body wouldn't let her.

"Mail for you." Annie handed Polly an envelope when she came downstairs one Saturday, ready for a run. The tour was kicking off the following week, and the dancer was building up her stamina to get through the rigorous eight-week travel and performance schedule. She took the letter that was thick and on the heavy side. Inside, was a wedding invitation, requesting her attendance at the wedding of Jenny and Mac, two months from now, at their property in Kentucky. It looked like Mac was ready to make an honest woman of Jenny as Jock had suggested in his apology speech. She handed the invitation to her mom who read it and looked up. "You going?"

"Nope," Polly said, as she took off on her run.

***

In week four of the tour, the StepWorks company arrived in Cincinnati for a three-night run. Tour performances were going well. Jay had honed the show, and reviews were good for the cast's rendition of the beloved musical that was always a fan favorite. Not long before the curtain was due to go up, Polly was in the dressing room getting ready. She had tied back her long hair and securely fastened the short black, bobbed wig on her head that helped transform her into Velma Kelly. She was putting the finishing touches to her exaggerated eye makeup, when a stagehand came in and announced there was a guy outside in the corridor who wanted to speak with her. "Who is it?" she asked, but the stagehand just shrugged. "Didn't say."

As Polly rounded a corner into the corridor, she found Marcus pacing. It took him a moment to recognize her through her disguise of a 1920's jazz baby, but when he did, he stepped forward to hug her. "I saw the tour was coming through Cincinnati, so I thought I'd drive up and cheer you on." Polly was tongue tied, overtaken by surprise, and unsure about how to react. She was secretly thrilled to see him but alarmed that he'd shown up without any warning.

"I'm sure you're busy getting ready," Marcus said, noticing her robe, "but I wondered if after the performance I could take you for dinner." He saw her frown. "Or maybe just a drink?"

"I have dinner plans with the cast," Polly said.

"Please, Polly," Marcus said plaintively. "We have to talk. I have to know what went wrong between us."

Polly couldn't deny that it was a fair request. He deserved to know how he'd blown it. "Okay," she said. "Meet me in the lobby after the show. I have to finish getting ready now." She turned and walked away.

When the curtain came up on the opening scene and her first big number of the show, Polly felt the nerves fluttering in her chest. Marcus was out there in the audience, watching. But as she heard the beginning notes of "All that Jazz", she pushed away her fears, until she was lost in concentration, belting out the song and shimmying across the stage in the dance she knew so well. As the song reached its crescendo, and she sang out its final defiant words, she heard the audience erupt in applause, and a persistent whistle that seemed to be coming from a particularly enthusiastic fan.

At show's end, as the curtain came down, the entire company was lined up across the stage to receive more loud cheers, whistles, and shouts of bravo. Polly was able to make out the figure of Marcus in the third row of the orchestra section. He was on his feet, clapping and cheering like his life depended on it.

Polly changed out of her costume, tamping down her excitement, forcing herself to slow down. Back in street clothes, she made her way to the lobby and spotted Marcus waiting for her. In one hand, he held a cap that he'd worn against the rain. In the other hand was a small bouquet of fragrant gardenias. After their time apart, it was like she was taking in his good looks for the first time, and flashing on what might have been between them felt like a gut punch. He handed her the flowers and went to take her arm, but she gently moved away from him. Outside, the rain had stopped. Marcus escorted her to a nearby restaurant he had scouted during the show's intermission. He heaped praise on her all along the way. She couldn't lie, it felt good to hear him fawn over her, lauding her talent, her amazing performance, and how great she had looked on stage. Once upon a time, Christian had done the same. He had marveled at her abilities, but then she had relinquished her power to him, and let her independence slip away. No doubt about it, a part of her was secretly happy that Marcus had traveled to see her. But it also unsettled her to feel him so near, virile and inviting, because she was sure a relationship with him was off the table. Giving up the hard-won independence she'd clawed back over the last couple of months was simply not in the cards.

Once they were seated and had ordered, Marcus reached across the table and took her hand. "What happened, Polly?"

She was stronger now and didn't need to protect herself by withholding her reasons, so she came clean. "You lied to me?"

"I never lied to you." Marcus was genuinely indignant.

Anger rose and colored her face. "Throughout our marriage, Christian lied to me. It's something I will no longer tolerate from any man." She looked directly at her dinner date, trying to keep it together.

"I swear to you, Polly, I did not lie to you."

She launched into the recriminations that had poisoned their promising relationship and killed it in the crib. "That first time you went to Kentucky, I went to your apartment. It was a Friday night and you were due back from your trip, so I went looking for you in the bar. When Sheri said you were in your apartment, I went up there to find you. Your front door was open, and when I went in, I saw Chrissy Reynolds lying on your bed, and she wasn't dressed for a picnic. She looked like she was ready for what you were planning to give her. She saw me, and I ran out before you could come in and see me standing there like an idiot, while

Chrissy brought the lingerie catalog to life." Polly confessed the incident in a rush, relieved to finally free herself of the festering upset.

"My god, Polly, is that what this has been about? The reason you cut me out? I've been going crazy trying to figure out what I did wrong."

"Yes," Polly said. "It's because you lied to me. If you'd told the truth and said that night, and any others you spent with Chrissy, didn't mean anything to you, I could have moved forward. Chrissy slept with my husband. She flaunted his text messages, and told me how he panted over her, and couldn't wait to get his hands on her, while I was at home, setting the table and cooking coq au vin, like some zoned-out Stepford Wife." Tears were coming now. "I keep thinking about what your mom said when Jock cheated on her, that nobody can make you feel inferior without your consent. Well, I'm not strong like her. Christian humiliated me, and I'll be damned if I let another man humiliate me again with a lie, especially a lie about another woman."

"Polly, I swear that I never slept with Chrissy Reynolds." Marcus was insistent, and Polly could see his face and voice were full of sincerity. "Before I ever knew that Christian was your husband, I watched him pawing Chrissy in the bar whenever they came in together. That Friday night, I was stuck in traffic and late getting back from my trip. You must have come and gone before I arrived home. Chrissy let herself into my unlocked apartment. I found her lying, uninvited, on my bed. Nothing about the way she behaved was seductive. She insulted me and cheapened herself with that stunt. I was furious, but I politely told her to leave and never to turn up unannounced again." There was a silence, as he waited for her reaction. "Please say you believe me, Polly. I adore you, and I've missed you so much. I can't believe you've let this keep us apart. Why didn't you tell me that you came by that night and saw Chrissy, so I could explain?"

Polly knew he was telling the truth. "Whenever I

confronted Christian about his lies, he just doubled down and told more," she said. "I'm sorry, Marcus. I've been confused and gun shy, and it didn't seem like such a hot idea to get involved with a new man at the same time I was kicking off a divorce."

After dinner, as Marcus walked her back to the hotel where she was staying, Polly let down her guard and leant against him. He wrapped a protective arm around her shoulders, and in the hotel lobby, he kissed her and held her close, as he whispered goodbye. "Jenny and Mac really want you to come to the wedding. Can I tell them you'll come?" he asked, his head bent so he could rest his forehead against hers.

"I'll be there," she said.

CHAPTER 17: UNFORGETABLE

The tour had finished and Polly was back home, sitting at the bar in Tres Caballeros with Danelle. While Polly had been away, her friend had driven down to the studio twice a week to cover classes for her. "I was bored being a stay-at-home mom twenty-four, seven," Danelle confessed. "The extra money has helped, and mama has officially got her groove back." Danelle shimmied on her barstool, while Polly laughed and raised her margarita. "Here's to your groove."

Polly felt a light tap on her shoulder and turned to see Chrissy Reynolds, who was dressed to kill, like a maneater on the prowl. "Hi, Polly," Chrissy said, looking over the dancer. Polly had come straight from teaching a dance class and now sat, makeup-free and a bit disheveled, sipping her drink. "Oh, hi Chrissy, this is my friend Danelle, and Danelle, *this* is Chrissy. Remember I told you about her?"

"I sure do." Danelle sucked hard on her straw to slurp up the margarita, watching Chrissy with a glint in her eye.

"I hear Christian and you are finalizing your divorce?" Chrissy said.

"That is true." Polly was once again bowled over by the strumpet's nerve. *This woman's stunt tripped me up and kept me from Marcus. But she's also the reason I'm ending my crackpot marriage to Christian, so I don't know whether to hug her or slug her.*

"Yeah, now Christian is all in my messages, trying to hook up again," Chrissy announced, smoothing her hair, which was pulled back into a sleek bun. She was in her signature tight pencil skirt, a silk blouse with a plunging neckline, and a pale gray wrap. "He's all over me like…"

"Flies on shit?" Danelle said, cutting the blonde off mid-sentence, before taking another long slurp of her cocktail.

"Classy," Chrissy hissed, throwing Danelle a dirty look.

"You should run along," Danelle said with a smile. "I'm sure Christian or some other guy is waiting for you in the toilet." Danelle flashed a smile at Chrissy, as Polly looked down and stifled a grin. She knew she should put a stop to her friend's snark, but it was too entertaining. Chrissy pulled her cashmere wrap a little tighter around her shoulders, obviously rattled by Danelle's commentary. "Any woman with two brain cells knows that Christian is only good for a fling. He's a male bimbo."

"So you completely broke it off with him?" Danelle asked, her eyes purposely wide and innocent.

"I dropped him like third-period French," Chrissy snarked.

"Good move." Danelle took another slurp of her drink, as she drained the last of the liquid and sucked loudly on the ice at the bottom of her glass. "And when you broke up with him, did you tell Christian about how you showed up uninvited to Marcus's place, and laid on his bed like a ho, until he put you out like trash?"

Chrissy narrowed her eyes, and Polly flashed her friend a look that warned her to knock it off. "Danelle!"

"What?" Danelle replied, wide-eyed again. She looked at Chrissy. "Polly is right. I'm being too harsh. Marcus only thought you were trash. He ran you out of his place in a classy way, like the Southern gentleman that he is."

Chrissy turned and walked away, leaving the two friends to sit in silence until she was out of earshot. Danelle set her empty glass on the bar and gestured for the bartender to bring them another round. "I'm not wrong," she said, looking at her friend with a shrug.

"You're not wrong," Polly agreed, and they both laughed.

***

Polly exited the terminal at the Cincinnati Northern Kentucky airport and immediately spotted Marcus's tall, unmistakable physique, as he waved at her with undisguised delight. They hugged, excited to reunite for such a special weekend. It was a warm afternoon in late September, and after only a ninety-minute drive, they arrived at his parent's farm. Polly caught sight of hired help. They were busy making final preparations for tomorrow's simple wedding ceremony, scheduled for 1:00 p.m. In the flower garden, at the back of the house, they'd set out a few rows of chairs, dressed with silk ribbons, to seat about thirty guests. Beyond the chairs, picnic tables had been covered with familiar blue-checked clothes and readied for the simple wedding luncheon that would follow the ceremony. Large mason jars filled with wild flowers would act as centerpieces.

In the kitchen, Polly found Jenny at the stove, stirring a soup, dressed in her chronic uniform of beat-up flannel shirt and jeans. She didn't look like a nervous bride-to-be. As her son walked in with his special guest, Jenny stopped stirring and limped over to hug her. "We're so happy you're here. Marcus said you were amazing in the show."

"Well, the tour is finished now and I'm not sure what's next." Polly smiled shyly and noticed how Jenny and Marcus exchanged knowing looks like co-conspirators.

***

Later that evening, after a quick and easy dinner of sandwiches and beer, Polly watched as Jenny expertly spread vanilla icing on her wedding cake. It was Mac's favorite, red velvet. In a vase, on the table, were six long-stemmed pink roses that the bride planned to turn into a bouquet by tying them with a simple white, silk ribbon. "What have you picked for your first dance?" Polly asked. Jenny and Mac turned to her with nonplussed expressions. "We hadn't thought about that," Mac said. "But we do have a bluegrass band with three fellas we know coming to play for us."

"Well it just so happens that choreographing wedding dances is my forte," Polly announced. Jenny looked at Mac. "Remember, years ago, when we were kids, Mac, there was a live band at the church hall? We danced to that song about a waltz?"

"'Tennessee Waltz'," Mac remembered.

"That's right," Jenny said.

"Your first dance will be a waltz then," Polly announced, as the betrothed couple shook their heads. "I've forgotten how to waltz if I ever knew," Mac said. "I'm sure, I just shuffled Jenny around the floor, tripping over my two left feet and stepping on her toes."

"Okay, both of you stand up. Marcus, you pull up 'Tennessee Waltz'," Polly ordered with the natural authority of a teacher. And there in the kitchen with Marcus beaming and the two labs, Piper and Bridie, watching from their dog beds, Polly taught Jenny and Mac how to waltz. Polly listened closely to the lyrics of the old song about a sweetheart that's taken by another. It was a fitting choice. Mac's sweetheart had been stolen away by Jock all those years ago, and tomorrow he was officially reclaiming her.

Polly and Marcus took a stroll after dinner and Polly asked if Jock was expected to attend the wedding. Marcus shook his head. "No, he's not coming. There's a limit to my father's graciousness. I think he's at peace with himself now that's he's tried to set things right with the family, but he couldn't bear to see Mac marry my mother because she was the love of his life."

"Even though he hurt her so much?"

"It's in no way a justification, but loving her so deeply is the reason he hurt her so much," Marcus said.

"So, you finally understand him?" Polly asked.

"Oh, I always understood him," Marcus said. "But sometimes, understanding is not enough. It's just the consolation prize."

She took his hand in hers and swung them as they walked. "How are things between your dad and you now?"

"They're okay. I'm living in the guest house at Turner-Bell, and Dad only has the stamina to work a couple of hours each day, if that. He leaves most of the running of the place to Dawson and me, so it's not like we're in each other's pockets. At night, I'm dog tired, so I eat alone, or Dawson might come by, and then I turn in, since we're up so early."

"It sounds like a good life," Polly said.

"It would be, if you were here with me." He leaned down and gently kissed her. "Come on, let's go in. Busy day tomorrow." She heard the longing in his voice. He wanted to make a life with her at Turner-Bell, but didn't want to linger too long on what he feared wasn't possible.

***

Sunday morning dawned warm and bright, a perfect September day of mellow sun and gentle breezes. Polly found Jenny in the kitchen making omelets. "Jenny, you're getting married in a few hours. Why aren't you doing some last-minute primping? Here, let me look at your hands." Jenny showed off her hands with their rough, chapped skin and broken nails. Polly examined them and looked up, slightly alarmed that the bride was being so loosey goosey about her big day. "Is anyone coming to do your hair and makeup?" Jenny shook her head with a grin.

"Okay, that's it," Polly said. "After breakfast I'm giving you a manicure, a makeover, and a blowout."

"I look that bad?" Jenny teased.

"You look fine for a work day, but today is your wedding day." Polly was surprised at how comfortable she was bossing her man's mother around. *Yes,* she thought, *he is my man now that there's no misunderstandings left to stumble over.* Jenny looked over at Mac and laughed. "I always knew I should have had a daughter."

After breakfast, Polly marched Jenny up to the master bedroom and ordered her into the shower. They had two hours for beautification before the ceremony began at one o'clock. When she emerged from her bathroom in a terry cloth robe, the lady of the house discovered that her young guest had spread out various beauty supplies on the dressing table. Polly proceeded to give the bride a mani-pedi, and when she had finished blowing on Jenny's nails to dry them, she looked up at her. "Show me the dress." Jenny pointed to a hanger on a door hook, where a pale blue dress in thick cotton was hanging, draped with a white mohair shawl. "That's lovely," Polly said, struck by the simple elegance of the outfit. She realized that today's wedding celebration was just a small step on Mac and Jenny's long journey. It was a bow they were tying on the love they had felt for each other for almost their whole lives, even when Jenny had been married to Jock and they couldn't be together.

Polly arranged the bride's hair in an elegant chignon and fixed it with a jeweled comb that Jenny retrieved from the bottom of a drawer. As she applied makeup to the older woman's handsome face, it was easy to see where Marcus had gotten his good looks. She lightly bronzed the strong forehead and high cheekbones. She applied a little lipstick, and despite Jenny's objections, Polly curled the older woman's lashes and applied two coats of mascara. "Perfume? Where's your perfume?" Polly asked, and Jenny pointed to a dusty bottle on the dresser that contained the dregs of an unidentifiable brown liquid. Polly removed the cap, squirted it and sniffed. "It looks old, but it smells good," she said, spraying it liberally around the bride. All done, she turned Jenny to face the mirror. "What do you

162

think?"

Jenny stared at herself in the glass and gave a small laugh. "Oh my sweet girl, thank you. I would never have thought to beat this old face into shape. Now I won't scare the guests."

"You look beautiful," Polly said and she meant it. Jenny was a naturally good-looking woman, and with a few simple embellishments, she'd been transformed into a stunner, befitting this special day. "Now put your dress on, while I bring your flowers up from the kitchen."

Polly watched Jenny arrange her roses into a simple bouquet, and set aside a single bud for Mac to wear in his lapel, before interrupting her. "Jenny?"

"Yes darlin'." Jenny smiled at her son's beautiful and thoughtful sweetheart.

"Why did Jock invite everyone to Turner-Bell that day and give a big speech?"

Jenny slowly wrapped white silk ribbon around the long stems of the roses. "Because I asked him to."

"I thought so." Polly had noticed Jenny giving her ex-husband a knowing look, urging him on, as though they had pre-arranged the whole thing together and she was his coach.

Jenny kept working on the flowers as she spoke. "I knew that Marcus would never come home until his father made amends for what he'd done. And it was breaking my boy's heart to be away from the farm. I was born and raised in horse country. I've been around horse people my whole life, and I never knew anyone to love horses and the horse business so much as Marcus. The first thing he saw when he came into this world was a gelding in a paddock." Jenny looked out the window at the horses grazing beyond. "I snatched him from the midwife, came outdoors in my nightdress, and in the early morning light, I laid his tiny body, all bundled up, on a horse's back."

Polly pictured the scene of the newborn being imprinted with the touch and smell of a horse, giving him that special bond she'd noticed whenever he was around the beautiful animals.

"Jock is stubborn," Jenny continued, tying the ends of the ribbon into a small bow. "But even he's not totally blind to reality or immune to consequences. It wouldn't surprise me if all that rage and bitterness he carried for years contributed to his cancer. It's good for him to atone and unload his guilty conscience. I daresay he feels better after doing it. He might even live longer. And now he has Marcus back." Jenny paused then looked deeply into Polly's eyes. "We all have him back." Polly understood her meaning. Marcus was hers for the taking.

***

At 1:00 p.m., the guests took their seats, and to the sweet sound of fiddling from the bluegrass band, Marcus and Dawson walked their mother down the small aisle. They handed her over to Mac, who was waiting for his bride, on a patch of grass that was strewn with rose petals, overcome by the moment and her beauty. Beaming and playful, the pair exchanged vows they had written themselves. With their life-long love story mostly behind them, they focused instead on their gratitude at being blessed with a love so strong and true that it had lasted, come what may, for so many years. Every guest gathered there for the nuptials knew the trials and tribulations that Mac Campbell and Jenny Turner had endured, so when the minister said, "You may kiss the bride," there was a loud cheer and not a dry eye in the place.

The wedding luncheon followed in the style of a country picnic, with a cooked, sliced ham, potato salad, fried chicken, mac and cheese, and a vegetable casserole, all topped off with Jenny's homemade red velvet cake. As the late afternoon came on, guests toasted the bride and groom with the good red and white wine that Mac had ordered for the occasion. Marcus was the last to give a toast. He stood, taking a deep breath and a long moment to gaze at his parents, as they sat, leaning against each other, at the wedding table. "Mac, I can only hope to be as good a man as you are. Mama, I can only hope to have a woman as wonderful and true as you. And so, here's to my inspiration, Jenny and Mac." As Marcus raised his glass to lead the toast, he caught Polly's eye and held it with a long, loving look. She winked at him, and then he watched in surprise, as she stood up and took her place next to the trio of bluegrass performers.

Dressed in her special rose-colored dress, her long, dark hair curled and tumbling over her bare shoulders, Polly stood on the grass with the band and began to sing 'Tennessee Waltz', her voice rich and clear. She had practiced with the musicians behind the stables so she might give an impromptu performance, as a wedding gift, for the happy couple, as they danced the waltz she had taught them. Mac helped Jenny to her feet, took her lovingly in his arms, and surrounded by their guests, he gently waltzed his sweetheart around the garden. Marcus watched his parents dance. Mac had waited almost his entire life for this moment when he could finally take Jenny Turner as his wife. As he looked beyond them to the beauty who was serenading them in the sweetest tones, Marcus had no intention of waiting any longer to take the woman he loved.

As evening fell, candles were lit, and the band played the lively bluegrass music that was famous in the region. The guests danced on, drinking and toasting, sharing old stories and fond memories. Seated next to Marcus in the wedding party, Polly looked around with a feeling of deep contentment. She was surround by the beauty of nature and all the blessings of a congenial life, as she luxuriated in the bosom of the fine family that had welcomed her so warmly. She felt Marcus caress her bare shoulder and run his hand down her arm. He moved aside her lush, dark hair to whisper in her ear. "Care to dance?" She stood, and they slow danced to the ballad the band was playing now that the evening was winding down and the mood was gentler and more romantic. Polly gave herself over to a joy that was building within her, as she felt her man's strong arms around her.

When the song finished, Marcus whispered, "Come with me." He took her by the hand and led her away from the party toward the quiet of the stable. Inside, they walked past the stalls where the horses softly neighed and snorted. He pointed to a ladder that led to an upper level of the barn. He climbed it first then reached for her hand to help her up. They were in the eaves on a large, straw-covered platform. The fading light and a soft breeze came in through an open window. On the floor, Polly saw Marcus had spread a large, soft, cotton comforter over the clean straw. In an ice bucket, was an opened bottle of champagne next to two flutes. Marcus sat on the comforter and patted where she should sit beside him. He poured two glasses of champagne and handed one to her. "To my woman who is like no other," he said, clinking her glass with his own.

"Thank you for today," he said, gently caressing her neck. His fingers trailed down to her breasts. "You helped make the day so special for Mac and my mother. She doesn't have much time to take care of herself, and she's never had a daughter to pamper her." His gaze locked with hers and she saw longing there. "In New York, I told you that when I made love to you, it would be at the perfect time in the perfect place and that you would never forget it." He tugged down the front of her dress, exposing her breasts so he could kiss them. He looked into her eyes as she opened her mouth slightly in anticipation. "This is the time and this is the place," Marcus said. He pulled off her dress, slipped off her shoes, and slid her panties down her long slim legs.

Polly could smell the warm, earthy aromas of the straw and it surprised her how erotic this simple venue could be. Below them, the horses stirred in their stalls. She had never seen Marcus dressed so elegantly before in dress pants and a crisp white shirt. Watching him walk his mother down the aisle, she had been filled with desire and wonder at how handsome he looked, his dark, curling hair combed back to show off his tanned face and fine features. She stared now as he unbuttoned his shirt, took it off, and slid his pants over his hips. He lay down beside her. "What do you want?" he asked.

"A kiss," she purred. Their awakened bodies knew what to do, and this time, there would be no stopping them. Their tongues touched, snaking around each other, their limbs entwined, until Polly could wait no more. She opened herself to him. "Please, take me, Marcus," she cried out.

***

As their bodies remained entwined in contented bliss, Marcus gently slid his hand up and down the length of her smooth belly. "What are you doing?" she asked.

"I'm checking," he said, "to see if there is room in there for a little girl who will grow up to wear a tutu and learn how to dance from her beautiful mother."

"What if she wants to ride horses?" Polly asked.

"I have that covered," Marcus said in her ear. Polly closed her eyes and whispered something under her breath. "What did you say, my love?" Marcus whispered in her ear. Polly looked into his loving eyes. "Unforgettable."

ACKNOWLEDGMENTS

Thanks to publisher Melissa Keir, Toni Kelley for her fine editing, and Emily at Fantasia Frog Designs for the cover art.

PENELOPE HOLT

ABOUT THE AUTHOR

Penelope Holt was born and educated in England and now lives in New York. She is a novelist, playwright, business writer, and marketing executive. Her work has been performed at the Edinburgh Fringe Festival, York Arts Center, and New York's American Folk Theater. In addition to writing fiction, which includes *The Women Who Want Series*, *The Angel Scroll*, and *The Apple*, based on the controversial Herman Rosenblat Holocaust romance, Holt is a prolific writer, editor, and co-author of non-fiction, including *Business Intelligence at Work A Personal Operating System for Career Success*, **Singing God's Work, the story of the Harlem Gospel Choir,** and many other works. She is married with two children.